1 MONTH OF
FREE
READING

at
www.ForgottenBooks.com

By purchasing this book you are eligible for one month membership to ForgottenBooks.com, giving you unlimited access to our entire collection of over 1,000,000 titles via our web site and mobile apps.

To claim your free month visit:
www.forgottenbooks.com/free315855

ISBN 978-0-365-20723-8
PIBN 10315855

This book is a reproduction of an important historical work. Forgotten Books uses
state-of-the-art technology to digitally reconstruct the work, preserving the original format
whilst repairing imperfections present in the aged copy. In rare cases, an imperfection in
the original, such as a blemish or missing page, may be replicated in our edition. We do,
however, repair the vast majority of imperfections successfully; any imperfections that
remain are intentionally left to preserve the state of such historical works.

Out of Doors
California and Oregon

By
J. A. Graves

Profusely Illustrated

Los Angeles
Grafton Publishing Co.
1912

COPYRIGHT
GRAFTON PUBLISHING COMPANY
1912

———

PRESS OF THE WEST COAST MAGAZINE
LOS ANGELES, CALIFORIA

CONTENTS

*T*o the memory of my sons

Selwyn Emmett Graves
and
Jackson A. Graves, Jr.

**Both of whom were nature lovers, this book
is lovingly dedicated.**

ILLUSTRATIONS

ILLUSTRATIONS—Continued

MOUNT PITT

A MOTOR TRIP IN SAN DIEGO'S BACK COUNTRY.

Come, you men and women automobilists, get off the paved streets of Los Angeles and betake yourselves to the back country of San Diego county, where you can enjoy automobile life to the utmost during the summer. There drink in the pure air of the mountains, perfumed with the breath of pines and cedars, the wild lilacs, the sweet-pea vines, and a thousand aromatic shrubs and plants that render every hillside ever green from base to summit. Lay aside the follies of social conditions, and get back to nature, pure and unadorned, except with nature's charms and graces.

To get in touch with these conditions, take your machines as best you can over any of the miserable roads, or rather apologies for roads, until you get out into the highway recently constructed from Basset to Pomona. Run into Pomona to Gary avenue, turn to the right and follow it to the Chino ranch; follow the winding roads, circling to the

Chino hills, to Rincon, then on, over fairly
good roads, to Corona. Pass through that
city, then down the beautiful Temescal Canyon to Elsinore. Move on through Murri-
etta to Temecula.

THREE ROUTES.

Beyond Temecula three routes are open
to you. By one of them you keep to the
left, over winding roads full of interest and
beauty, through a great oak grove at the
eastern base of Mt. Palomar. Still proceeding through a forest of scattering oaks, you
presently reach Warner's ranch through a
gate. Be sure and close all gates opened by
you. Only vandals leave gates open when
they should be closed.

Warner's ranch is a vast meadow, mostly
level, but sloping from northeast to southwest, with rolling hills and sunken valleys
around its eastern edge. A chain of mountains, steep and timber-laden, almost en-
circles the ranch. For a boundary mark on
the northeastern side of the ranch, are steep,
rocky and forbidding looking mountains.
Beyond them, the desert. The ranch comprises some 57,000 acres, nearly all valley
land. It is well watered, filled with lakes,

[2]

springs, meadows and running streams, all draining to its lowest point, and forming the head waters of the San Luis Rey River.

You follow the road by which you enter the ranch, to the left, and in a few miles' travel you bring up at Warner's Hot Springs, a resort famed for many years for the curative properties of its waters. The springs are now in charge of Mr. and Mrs. Stanford, and are kept in an admirable manner, considering all of the difficulties they labor under. The run from Los Angeles to the springs is about 140 miles, and can be made easily in a day. Once there, the choice of many interesting trips is open to you.

PAST TEMECULA.

After leaving Temecula, another road much frequented by the autoists is the right-hand road by the Red Mountain grade to Fallbrook, either to Del Mar, by way of Oceanside, or into the Escondido Valley by way of Bonsal, Vista and San Marcos. The third route, the center one between those I have described, leads to Pala. With a party of five in a six-cylinder Franklin car, I went over the latter route on April 20th, 1911.

Every inch of the road was full of interest. We passed through Pala, with its ancient mission of that name, and its horde of Indian inhabitants. The children of the Indian school were having a recess, and they carried on just about in the same manner that so many "pale-faced" children would. Leaving Pala, we followed the main road along the left bank of the San Luis Rey River— where the San Diego Highway Commission is now doing work, which will, when finished, bring one to Warner's ranch by an easy grade—until we had gotten a few miles into the Pauma rancho. We crossed the Pauma Creek, and some distance beyond it we left the river to our right, turned sharply to the left, and ran up to the base of Smith's, or Palomar Mountain. Then came the grade up the mountain.

If you are not stout-hearted, and haven't a powerful machine, avoid this beautiful drive. If you are not driving an air-cooled car, carry extra water with you. You will need it before you reach the top. The road is a narrow zigzag, making an ascent of 4000 feet in a distance of from ten to twelve miles of switch-backing around the face of a steep rock-ribbed mountain. To add to its difficulties, the turns are so short that a long car is compelled to back up to negotiate them. About an hour and a quarter is required to make the trip up the mountain. We did all of it on low gear. When the top is finally reached, the view of the surrounding country is simply beyond description.

BELATED SPRING.

The mountain oaks of great size and broad of bough, were not yet fully in leaf. Pines and cedars, and to my astonishment, many large sycamores, were mingled with the oaks. A gladsome crop of luscious grasses covered the earth. Shrubs and plants were bursting into bloom. As we moved on we saw several wild pigeons in graceful flight among the trees. After traveling the backbone of the mountain for some distance we came to a dimly marked trail, leading to the left. The "Major Domo" of our party said that this road led to Doane's Valley, and that we must go down it. It was a straight up and down road, with exceedingly abrupt pitches, in places damp and slippery, and covered with fallen leaves. At the bottom of the descent, which it would have been impossible to retrace, we came to a small stream. Directly in the only place where we could have crossed it a log stuck up, which rendered passage impossible. After a deal of prodding and hauling, we dislodged it and safely made the ford.

Doane's Valley is one of those beauty spots which abound in the mountains of California. Its floor is a beautiful meadow, in which are innumerable springs. Surrounding this meadow is heavy timber, oaks, pines and giant cedars. Pauma Creek flows out of this meadow through a narrow gorge, which nature evidently intended should some day be closed with a dam to make of the valley a reservoir to conserve the winter waters. We followed a partially destroyed road through the meadow to its upper end. Then as high and dry land was within sight we attempted to cross a small, damp, but uncertain looking waterway.

WHEELS STUCK.

The front wheels passed safely, but when the rear wheels struck it they went into the mud until springs and axles rested on the ground. Two full hours we labored before we left that mud hole. We gathered up timbers and old bridge material, then jacked

[6]

up one wheel a little way, and got something under it to hold it there. The other side was treated the same way. By repeating the operation many times we got the wheels high enough to run some timbers crosswise beneath them. We put other timbers in front and pulled out.

We soon reached Bailey's Hotel, a summer resort of considerable popularity. We continued up the grade until we came onto the main road left by us when we descended into Doane's Valley. We got up many more pigeons, graceful birds, which the Legislature of our State should protect before they are exterminated. We moved on through heavily timber-covered hills, up and down grade, and finally came out on the south side of the mountain overlooking the canyon, some 5000 feet deep, at the bottom of which ran the San Luis Rey River. What would have been a most beautiful scene was marred by a fog which had drifted up the canyon. But the cloud effect was marvelous. We were above the clouds. A more perfect sky no human being ever saw. The clouds, or fog banks, were so heavy that it looked as if we could have walked off into them. I never saw similar cloud effects anywhere else except from Mt. Lowe, near Los Angeles, and Mt. Tamalpais, in Marin County.

WARNER'S RANCH.

We now began our descent to Warner's Ranch. It was gradual enough for some distance, and the road and trees were as charming as any human being could desire. Finally we came out onto a point overlooking the ranch. The view was simply entrancing. Imagine a vast amphitheater of 57,000 acres, surrounded by hills, dotted here and there with lakes, with streams of water like threads of burnished silver glittering in the evening light, softened by the clouds hanging over the San Luis Rey River. There were no clouds on the ranch; they stopped abruptly at the southwest corner. This vast meadow was an emerald green, studded with brilliant colored flowers. Vast herds of cattle were peacefully completing their evening meal. The road down to the ranch follows a ridge, which is so steep that no machine has ever been able to ascend it. I held my breath and trusted to the good old car that has done so much for my comfort, safety and amusement. We were all glad when the bottom was reached. We forded the river and whirled away to Warner's Hot Springs, over good meadow roads, arriving there before 7 o'clock p. m.

Some day these springs are going to be appreciated. Now only hardy travelers, as a rule, go there. Their medicinal qualities will in time be realized, and the people of Southern California will find that they have a Carlsbad within a short distance of Los Angeles, in San Diego County. We slept the sleep of the tired, weary tourist that night.

HOT BATHS.

The following day we passed in bathing in the hot mineral waters, sightseeing and driving around the valley.

Saturday morning at 7:30 o'clock we bade adieu to Mr. and Mrs. Stanford and left the ranch by way of the Rancho Santa Isabel. The rain god must have been particularly partial to this beautiful ranch this season. Nowhere on our trip did we see such a splendid growth of grass and flowers, such happy looking livestock, such an air of plenty and prosperity as we did here. Leaving the ranch at the Santa Isabel store, we took the Julian road, which place we reached after a few hours' riding over winding roads good to travel on, and through scenery which was a constant source of enjoyment. Julian is one of the early settlements of San Diego County. Mining has been carried on there with varying successes and disappointments these many years. Now apple raising is its great industry. The hillsides are given over to apple culture.

The trees are now laden with blossoms. As we topped a hill or crossed a divide before beginning an ascent or descent, the view backward of the apple orchards, peeping up over slight elevations in the clearings, was extremely beautiful. Leaving Julian, we whirled along over splendid roads through a rolling country, given over to fruit farming, stock raising and pasturage. We next reached Cuyamaca and visited the dam of that name, which impounds the winter rains for the San Diego Flume Company. The country around the lake showed a deficiency of rainfall.

The lake was far from full. We took our lunch at the clubhouse near the dam. After resting in the shade of the friendly oaks we then pursued our journey to Descanso. We passed through Alpine and finally entered the El Cajon Valley, famed far and wide for its muscatel grapes, which seem especially adapted to its dark red soil. The vines were in early leaf, and not as pleasing to the eye as they will be when in full bloom. Then came Bostonia, a comparatively new settlement, Rosamond, La Mesa, and finally we whirled off on a splendid road, through an unsettled country overgrown with sage and shrubs, to Del Mar.

The sky was overcast all the afternoon. A stiff ocean breeze blew inland, cool and refreshing. The entire day had been spent amid scenes of rare beauty. The wild flowers are not yet out in profusion, but enough were there to give the traveler an idea of what can be expected in floral offerings later in the season. It was early Spring wherever the elevation was 3500 feet or better. The oaks were not yet in leaf, the sycamores just out in their new spring dresses, the wild pea blossoms just beginning to open and cast their fragrance to the breezes.

FAR BELOW.

Yellow buttercups adorned the warmer spots in each sunny valley. Way below us in the open country great fields of poppies greeted the gladdened eye. The freshness of spring was in the air. Each breath we inhaled was full of new life. The odor of the pines mingled its fragrance with that of the apple blossoms.

Del Mar is the Del Monte of Southern California. We arrived at Stratford Inn, at that place, which is as well furnished and as well kept as any hotel on the Coast. A small garden, an adjunct of the hotel, shows what the soil and climate of Del Mar is capable of producing. Tomato vines are never frosted. The vegetables from the garden have a fresher, crisper taste than those grown in a drier atmosphere. How good and comfortable the bed felt to us that night! Sleep came, leaving the body inert and lifeless in one position for hours at a time. The open air, the sunshine, the long ride, the ever changing scenery, brought one joyous slumber, such as a healthy, happy, tired child enjoys.

The next morning, after an ample, well-cooked and well-served breakfast, we took the road on the last leg of our journey. Over miles and miles of newmade roads we sped. Soon the long detour up the San Luis Rey Valley will be a thing of the past. The new county highway will pursue a much more direct course. We passed through miles of

CUYAMACA LAKE, NEAR PINE HILLS

EL CAJON VALLEY, SAN DIEGO, FROM SCHUMANN-HEINK
POINT, GROSSMONT.

land being prepared for bean culture. Miles of hay and grain, miles of pasturage, in which sleek cattle grazed peacefully, or, having fed their fill, lay upon the rich grasses and enjoyed life. Near the coast the growth of grain and grass far surpasses that of the interior.

Santa Marguerita Rancho, with its boundless expanse of grass-covered pasturage lands, its thousands of head of cattle and horses, its thousands of acres of bean lands, ready for seed, is worth going miles to see.

At noon we reached San Juan Capistrano. We drove into the grounds of the hospitable Judge Egan. At a table, beneath the grateful shade of giant trees, amid the perfume of flowers, the sweet songs of happy birds, we ate our lunch. After a short rest we took up the run again. We passed El Toro and finally came onto the great San Joaquin ranch, every acre of which is now highly cultivated.

Then came the Santa Ana region, thickly settled, rich in soil and products. We passed through beautiful and enterprising Santa Ana, through miles upon miles of walnut, orange and other fruit groves, through a solid settlement extending far on each side of the road, to Anaheim. And still on through more walnut and orange groves, more wealth-producing crops.

Through the orange and lemon and walnut groves of Fullerton, extending to and forming a large part of Whittier, I could not help exclaiming to myself, "What an empire this is! Where is the country that yields the annual returns per acre that this land does?" At Whittier we got into one of the newly constructed county highways, and at 3:30 p. m. we were home again, after four days in the open, four days of pure and unadulterated happiness.

IN SAN DIEGO COUNTY

SAN DIEGO MOUNTAIN SCENE

A HUNTING TRIP IN THE LONG AGO

One of the disadvantages of old age, even advancing years, is the pleasure we lose in anticipating future events. Enthusiastic youth derives more pleasure in planning a journey, an outing or a social gathering than can possibly be realized from any human experience. With what pleasure the young set out, getting ready for a hunting trip, or an excursion to some remote locality never visited by them!

From the first day I arrived in Los Angeles, I had heard of the Fort Tejon and the Rancho La Liebre country as a hunting paradise, extolled by all people I met, who were given to spending an occasional week or two in the mountains in search of game. In consequence of what I had heard of this region, I made up my mind to go there the first time I got an opportunity.

Among the first acquaintances I made here was a dear old man named A. C. Chauvin, formerly of St. Louis, Mo., and of French descent. He had spent many years in the Northwest, hunting and trapping. He was an excellent shot with both rifle and shotgun. Notwithstanding the fact that he was slightly afflicted with a nervous disorder akin to palsy, which kept his left arm and hand, when not in use, constantly shaking, the moment he drew up his gun, his nerves were steady, and his aim perfect. He despised the modern breech-loading rifle, and insisted on shooting an old-fashioned, muzzle-loading, single-barrel rifle, made by a fellow townsman, Henry Slaughterbach. It was an exceedingly accurate and powerful shooting gun. Chauvin was a thorough hunter, well versed in woodcraft, up in camp equipage and the requirements of men on a two or three weeks' hunting trip.

OFF IN THE DUST.

During the summer of 1876 I had been hard at work. The weather had been hot and trying. In the latter part of September, Mr. Chauvin proposed that I go with him on a deer hunt to the Liebre Ranch. I was practicing law, and after consulting my partners, I eagerly consented to accompany him. He made all the preparations. On the 30th of September he started a two-horse wagon, loaded with most of our outfit, on

[16]

ahead, in charge of a roustabout. On October 2nd, we followed in a light one-horse wagon, taking with us our blankets, a few provisions and a shotgun. We had a hard time pulling over the grade beyond San Fernando, but finally made it. We went on past Newhall, and camped the first night on the bank of the Santa Clara River.

Without the slightest trouble we killed, within a very few minutes, enough quail for supper and breakfast. After we had finished our evening meal, quite a shower came up very suddenly. Just enough rain fell to make things sticky and disagreeable. The clouds vanished and left as beautiful a starlit sky as any human being ever enjoyed. Our wagon had a piece of canvas over it, which shed the rain, and left the ground beneath the wagon dry. Upon this spot we spread our blankets and went to sleep. Next morning the sun got up, hot, red and ugly looking. We breakfasted, hitched up and started up San Francisquito Canyon. Chauvin remarked we were in for a hot day, and he proved a good prophet. There wasn't a breath of wind stirring as the day progressed. The heat fairly sizzled. A goodly part of the road was well shaded. We were loath to leave the shady spots when we came to the open places. To lighten our load we walked most of the way. We stopped for lunch, fed and rested our weary animal, and just at dark after a weary afternoon's work we reached Elizabeth Lake, where we overtook the other wagon. We had been two full days on the road. I have made the same trip in an automobile two summers in succession, in less than four hours.

IN ANTELOPE COUNTRY.

On leaving Elizabeth Lake next morning we transferred everything of any weight from our wagon to the larger one, which made the going much easier for our animal. We descended the hill beyond the lake, went up the valley a few miles, and then cut straight across to a point near where Fairmont is now situated. Chauvin said he wanted to get an antelope before going after the deer. We crossed the valley into some low, rolling hills and camped on a small stream called Rock Creek. Chauvin said this was a great place for antelope. The horses were picketed out on a grassy cienega, which offered them pretty good feed. We got our supper, made camp and went to bed.

FERN BRAKE, PALOMAR MOUNTAIN

THE MARGARITA RANCH HOUSE

During the night a wind began to blow from the northwest, and in a few hours it had become a hurricane. Small stones were carried by it like grains of sand. They would pelt us on the head as we lay in our blankets. We could hear the stones clicking against the spokes of the wagon wheels. Great clouds of dust would obscure the sky. By morning the velocity of the wind was terrific. Our horses, driven frantic, had broken loose and disappeared. We could not make a fire, nor if we had had one could we have cooked anything, for the dirt that filled the air. For breakfast we ate such things as we had prepared. The roustabout started off trailing the horses. Chauvin and I sat around under a bank, blue and disconsolate.

About 11 o'clock we saw a great band of antelope going to water. They were coming up against the wind, straight to us. When fully half a mile away they scented us and started off in a circle to strike the creek above us. We put off after them, following up the creek bed. They beat us to it, watered and started back to their feeding ground, passing us in easy range. We shot at them, but without effect. The wind blew so hard that accurate shooting was an impossibility. We went back to camp. Not far from it we found quite a hole under the bank, which the winter waters had burrowed out. It afforded shelter enough from the wind, which was still blowing, to allow us to build a fire of dry sage brush. We then prepared a good, warm meal, which we ate with great relish. By 1 o'clock in the afternoon the wind began to abate, and it died away almost as suddenly as it came up. It left the atmosphere dry and full of dust.

GREAT SIGHT.

We heard nothing from the man who had gone after the horses. About 3 o'clock Chauvin said he was going to get an antelope or know why. He argued that they would be coming to water soon. He told me to remain near the camp. He went up the stream, intending to get above the point at which the animals usually watered. He had been gone about an hour, when I saw the dust rise toward the east—such a dust as a drove of sheep in motion makes. Pretty soon the advance guard of the largest band of antelope I ever saw, or ever hope to see again, appeared in sight. As they scented our

DIEGO AND CORONADO ISLANDS FROM GROSSMONT

GRADE ON PALOMAR MOUNTAIN

camp, what a sight they made! There they stood, out of range, looking to the point where their keen noses notified them that danger lurked. Then they would wheel and run, stop and look again. The white spots on their rumps shone in the sunlight like burnished silver.

They would stop, look awhile and again wheel and run. Suspicious and anxious they stood, heads up and nostrils dilated, sides heaving. They made a beautiful picture of excited and alarmed curiosity. Several times they advanced, and then fell back. Finally they whirled away and headed up stream. In a few minutes I heard the report of Chauvin's rifle, followed a little later by another shot. Then the whole band appeared in wild disorder, running as only frightened antelopes can run, in the direction from which they came. Shortly afterwards I saw Chauvin on a little knoll. I waved my arms. He saw me, took off his hat and beckoned for me to join him. Off I put, as fast as my legs could carry me. When I got to him, I found he had killed two antelope bucks. They lay within 400 yards of each other. He had already cut their throats.

Maybe you think we were not happy! We drew the animals. Chauvin was an old man, compactly built, but very strong. He helped me shoulder the smaller of the bucks, and then he, with the greatest ease, picked up the other one, and we trudged to camp. We hung our game up on a couple of stunted stumps and skinned them. Then we prepared supper. We cooked potatoes and rice, made coffee, and cornbread, and fried the antelope livers with bacon. Just as our meal was ready, our roustabout came into camp, riding one of the horses barebacked, with only a halter and leading the other two. He had had his hat blown away and was bareheaded. He was nearly frozen, having started off in the morning without his coat.

HORSES RECOVERED.

He trailed the horses, which were traveling before the wind, for twelve miles. Fortunately at a point on the south side of the valley, they entered a ravine, in which there was plenty of bunch grass. Here, sheltered from the wind, they fed up the ravine a mile or so, where he found them lying down in a sheltered spot near a water hole. He had

had nothing to eat since leaving us. Coming back he faced the wind until it died away. Riding a horse bareback, with a halter for a bridle, and leading two other horses, you can well imagine was no picnic. We tied the animals to some willow stumps, so there was no danger of their getting loose, and gave them a feed of barley. By this time the roustabout was thawed out by our fire, and we had supper.

As we had all the antelope we wanted, we made our plans for the next day. Chauvin knew the country thoroughly. He proposed that the next morning we go to where the horses had been found, and proceed up that canyon onto the Liebre ranch to a camping spot he knew of. He was certain we would find deer there. At peace with the world, we went to bed that night well fed and contented. Next morning we had antelope steak, right out of the loin, for breakfast. I never tasted better meat but once, and that was a moose steak served us one morning at the Hotel Frontenac in Quebec a few years ago.

We broke camp early. About noon time we had crossed the valley and gained our new camp, which was an ideal one. There was a spring of hot and a spring of cold iron and sulphur water within ten feet of each other, each near a stream of cold, clear mountain water. The first thing we did was to take a bath in the hot sulphur water. There was quite a hole in which it boiled up. It was almost too hot for comfort, but how cleansing it was! It took all of the sand out of our hair and beard and eyes, and left the skin as soft as satin. After our hot bath, we cooled off in the stream and got into our clothes. Refreshed and encouraged, we were extremely happy.

DEER PLENTIFUL.

Deer tracks were very plentiful. We fixed up our camp, cut up our antelope, put a lot of it out to dry or "jerk," as the common expression is, and then about an hour before sunset, Chauvin and I set out to look the country over. There was plenty of timber, pinons and other pines, and oaks, scrub and large, all full of acorns, upon which the deer were feeding. Returning from camp, not 100 yards from it, we jumped two bucks. We killed both of them, each getting one. Just about then, we began to think things were coming our way. We drew the deer, and in hanging them up on a small oak tree,

I pressed a yellow-jacket with the middle finger of my right hand. Before I got the stinger out, my upper lip swelled up to enormous proportions, and both my eyes were swollen shut. Chauvin looked at me with open-eyed and open-mouthed astonishment. In a characteristic tone, native to him, he remarked, "If I hadn't seen it, I couldn't believe it." He had to lead me to camp.

I have been very susceptible to bee stings all my life. Several years before this a bumble bee had stung me on my upper lip, and my whole face was swollen out of shape for many days. I suppose that fact had something to do with the peculiar action of this sting. At any rate, I was in great misery, and lay in camp with my eyes swollen shut for three days before the swelling began to abate. I drank great quantities of the sulphur water, and bathed my face in it continuously.

The morning after the yellow-jacket incident, Chauvin and the roustabout, the latter taking my gun, left me in bed and went out after deer. They left without breakfast, about daylight. Shortly afterwards, two of the horses broke loose and ran through camp terror stricken. The third horse strained at his stake rope, but did not break it. He snorted and stamped at a great rate. The loose horses did not leave camp, but kept up a constant running and snorting for some time. When Chauvin came back, he found that a bear had come down from the mountains near by, torn down and partially devoured one of the deer we had killed the night before, not one hundred yards from where I lay in bed.

Don Elogio de Celis, a well known citizen of Los Angeles, was camped in a canyon about a mile west of us. That afternoon he killed a grizzly bear of pretty good proportions, and we all supposed that he was the marauder who had visited our camp that morning.

While I was laid up Chauvin got two more bucks, several tree squirrels and some mountain quail. We made plenty of jerky, while living off the fat of the land.

About four or five days after I was stung, the swelling went down sufficiently for me to see again, but I had lost my appetite for further hunting, especially as Chauvin had had several long tramps without any luck. We stayed in camp a couple of days longer, then, as signs of a rainstorm were prevalent, we packed up and left camp very early one morning, and the first day got back to Newhall. The next morning, when we reached San Fernando, as I was not feeling any too well, I took the train for Los Angeles, so as to avoid the hot, dusty ride in by wagon.

For many months Chauvin repeated to our friends the extraordinary circumstances of my lip and eyes swelling up from a yellow-jacket's sting on the finger. He had hunted and trapped all his life, but could not get over that one incident.

What we had expected to be a pleasant outing proved to be rather a hard experience, but we were too old at the game not to have enjoyed it, and do you realize that after we got rested up, we felt better for our experience? Life in the open, the change of air, the excitement of hunting, all united in sweeping the cobwebs from our brains and left us better prepared for the battle of life than we were before we started.

PROFESSOR "LO," PHILOSOPHER

My Interview with an Educated Indian in the Wilds of Oregon:

In the summer of 1902 I was camping, in company with the late Judge Sterry of Los Angeles, on Spring Creek in the Klamath Indian Reservation in Southeast Oregon. Spring Creek rises out of lava rocks and flows in a southeasterly direction, carrying over 200,000 inches of the clearest, coldest water I ever saw. In fact, its waters are so clear that the best anglers can only catch trout, with which the stream abounds, in riffles, that is where the stream runs over rocks of such size as to keep the surface in constant commotion, thus obscuring the vision of the fish.

Two miles, or thereabouts, from its source, Spring Creek empties into the Williamson River. The Williamson rises miles away in a tule swamp, and its waters are as black as black coffee. Where the two streams come together, the dark waters of the Williamson stay on the left hand side of the stream, go-

RESTLY AT KLAMATH LAKE

ing down, and the clear waters of Spring
Creek on the right hand side, for half a mile
or more. Here some rapids, formed by a
swift declivity of the stream, over sunken
boulders, cause a mix-up of the light and
dark waters, and from there on they flow
intermingled and indistinguishable.

Nine miles down stream, the Sprague
River comes in from the left. It is as large
as the Williamson, and its waters are the
color of milk, or nearly so. The stream flows
for miles over chalk beds and through chalk
cliffs, which gives its waters their weird coloring. The union of the waters of the Williamson and the Sprague Rivers results in
the dirty, gray coloring of the waters of
Klamath Lake, into which they empty, and
of the Klamath River, which discharges the
lake into the Pacific Ocean.

KILLICAN.

The place where the Williamson is joined
by the Sprague is known as the "Killican."
The stream here flows over a lava bottom
and is quite wide, in places very deep and
in places quite shallow. There seemed to be
quite an area of this shallow water. The
shallow places suddenly dropped off into

pools of great depth, and it was something of a stunt to wander around on the shallow bed rock and cast off into the pools below. I tried it and found the lava as smooth and slippery as polished glass.

After sitting down a couple of times in water two feet deep, I concluded to stay on shore and cast out into the pool. Following this exhilarating exercise with indifferent success, I noticed approaching a little, old Indian. He was bareheaded and barefooted. His shirt was open, exposing his throat and breast. His eyes were deep set, his hair and beard a grizzly gray. He had a willow fishing pole in one hand and a short bush with green leaves on it, with which he was whacking grasshoppers, in the other. He circled around on the bank near me, now and again catching a hopper. I noticed that he ate about two out of every five that he caught. The others he kept for bait.

Finally he approached the stream. He paid no attention whatever to me. He selected a spot almost under me, squatted down upon a flat rock, put two grasshoppers on his hook, threw it into the stream, and in a very short time drew out a good six-pound trout. Filled with admiration for the feat,

A PRAIRIE HOMESTEAD

while he was tying a string through the fish's gills I said to him, "Muy mahe," which another Indian had told me meant "big trout." Without looking up or turning his head, he said to me in perfect English, "What sort of lingo are you giving me, young man? The true pronunciation of those words is," and then he repeated "Muy mahe," with just a little twist to his words that I had not given them. Resuming the conversation he remarked, "Why not speak English? When both parties understand it, it is much more comfortable. I intended to catch but one fish, but as you have admired this one, allow me to present it to you with my compliments." He had turned around now, and held out the struggling trout, a pleasant smile upon his worn features.

Embarrassed beyond measure, I apologized for attempting to talk to him in his own language, and accepted the trout. He baited his hook, cast it into the stream, and in a short time landed a still larger trout. Without removing it from the hook, he came up the bank to where I was seated. He laid his fish and rod on the grass, wiped his forehead with his hand and sat down.

"I never catch more fish, or kill more game

than I need for my present wants," he re-marked. "That trout will be ample for my wife and myself for supper and breakfast, and in fact for all day tomorrow. When he is gone, I will catch another one."

Then, turning to me, he asked, "From what section of civilization do you hail?" I told him I was from Los Angeles.

"Ah, Los Angeles," he murmured. "The Queen City of the West and Angel City of the South. I have read much of your beautiful city, and I have often thought I would like to visit it and confirm with my own eyes all I read about it. What a paradise that country must have been for the Indian before you white men came! I can hardly imagine a land of perpetual sunshine, a land where the flowers bloom constantly, where snows never fall. Yes, I would like to go there, but I imagine I never shall." Then, with an inquiring glance, "What may be your calling?" he asked.

I told him I was an attorney-at-law.

"A noble profession," he remarked. "Next to medicine I regard it as the noblest profession known to our limited capabilities. Do you ever think," he asked me, "that the medical profession is devoted to relieving

KLAMATH LAKE AND LINK RIVER

physical ills? To warding off death? The law, on the other hand, takes care of your property rights. It is supposed to be the guardian of the weak. How often, however, do we see its mission perverted, and how often it becomes an oppressor of the unfortunate. How many times do we see it aiding in the accumulation of those large fortunes with which our modern civilization is fast becoming burdened and brutalized."

While I had never contracted the filthy habit of smoking, I had in my pocket several good cigars. I extended the case to my new-found friend. He took one, thanked me, bit off the end, lit it and puffed away with evident enjoyment. I took the liberty of asking him his business. "I am a professor of belles lettres and philosophy in the Indian College on the Klamath reservation. I am here on my vacation. I was born and reared to early manhood in these mountains. They still have a charm for me. While I love my books and my labors, there is a freedom in my life here which appeals to me. Here I go back to natural life, and study again the book of nature. Each day I take a lesson from the wild animals of the forest, from the surging streams and twittering birds. Here I can better realize how small is man in the general plan of creation."

He hesitated, and I took advantage of his silence and asked him about the religion of his race. Whether the modern red man adhered to the teachings of his tribe, or leaned toward the white man's God. Replying, he delivered to me a discourse of considerable length, which, as near as I can recollect it now, ran as follows:

A RED AGNOSTIC.

"My people have been too busy these many years filling their stomachs to pay much attention to saving their souls. We teach a religion that inculcates good behavior, and promises as a reward for a well-spent life an eternity of bliss in the happy hunting ground. Our future is depicted by our priests as a materialistic future, where we follow the chase, defeat our enemies and enjoy to our full those things which render us happy in this world. Personally, I have long since discarded the teachings of my people, and I am in a state of doubt which seriously perplexes me. I have read much and widely on this subject. I find that you white men have not one religion, but many.

SPRING CREEK

You are divided into sects, torn by factions. From the teachings of history I would think that the multitude of denominations you support was your greatest safeguard. You know from times past, when a religion becomes too powerful it becomes also intolerant, and persecutions follow. I am loath to accept the Christian theory of the origin of man or his probable destiny. Science teaches us that the human being has existed for millions of years longer than the churches admit we have existed. The idolatry practiced by the Catholic church repulses me, and yet its stability has strongly appealed to me. You will remember what Macaulay, in reviewing Ranke's History of the Popes, said of this church. After reviewing its history, its defeats and its triumphs, he added: 'And she may still exist in undiminished vigor when some traveler from New Zealand shall in the midst of a vast solitude take his stand on a broken arch of London Bridge to sketch the ruins of St. Paul.' And yet, neither the age of the church nor its stability is conclusive to my mind of its divine origin. I am rather convinced from these facts that it has been governed by a skillful set of men, who were able politicians and financiers, as well as religious enthusiasts. Certainly no protestant church can lay claim to divine origin. We know too well that the Episcopal church was founded by an English King, because the Pope of Rome refused him a divorce. Luther quarreled with his church and broke away from its restraints. Wesley founded the Methodist church, Calvin the Presbyterian church. The more I study the religious history of the world, the more I am convinced that religion is founded on fear. The immortal bard, from whom nothing seems to have been hidden, lays down the foundation of all religion in those words from 'Hamlet,' where he makes the melancholy Dane exclaim:

> "To die:—to sleep,—
> To sleep! perchance to dream:—ay, there's the rub;
> For in that sleep of death what dreams may come,
> When we have shuffled off this mortal coil,
> Must give us pause."

"Do you realize that Ingersoll, by his teachings and his denunciations of what he termed the 'absurdities of orthodox religious beliefs,' has done more toward shaking faith in many church doctrines than any man of this age? And, after all, is not his doctrine

WOOD RIVER, OREGON

a sane one? He says, in effect: 'I can not believe these things. My reason revolts at them. They are repugnant to my intellect. I can not believe that a just God will punish one of His creatures for an honest opinion.' He denies that there is such a God as the churches hold out to us. He denies that the world was created in six days; that man was created in the manner described in the Bible, and that woman was created from man's rib. He denies that miracles were ever performed, or that there was any evidence, reliable or authoritative, that they were ever performed. And yet he does not deny the existence of a future life. His doctrine on this point is, 'I know only the history of the past and the happenings of the present. I do not know, nor does any man know, anything of the future. Let us hope there is a life beyond the grave.'

"The old poet, Omar, argues against a future life. You will recall these lines:

" 'Strange, is it not, that of the multitudes who
  Before us pass'd the door of Darkness through,
    Not one returns to tell us of the Road,
  Which to discover we must travel, too.' "

"The churches tell us we must have faith

to be saved, but the great minds of the present age are not satisfied, any more than many of the great minds of the past were satisfied, to admit as a matter of faith the whole foundation of the Christian religion.

"People want to be shown. They are not willing to rely upon poorly authenticated stories of what occurred several thousand years ago. The question presents itself to us: Is the world better, for its present beliefs than it formerly was, when religion was a matter of statute? People may not be as religious as they once were, but they are certainly more humane. Women are no longer slaves, chattels, with unfeeling husbands. Slavery itself no longer exists in any civilized nation. Polygamy is not practiced to the extent that it was in Biblical days. The world progressed as fear ceased to rule the human mind.

"But, pardon me," he added with infinite grace and a charming wave of his hand, "you see your question has aroused in me the failing of the pedagogue. I have said more than I had intended."

"How do your people," I asked, "look upon the material progress of the age?"

"They are astounded," he answered. "Since

THE KILLICAN

the Modoc War many of my people have prospered. You have seen their farms, their houses, and noted their occupations. They are rich in lands and stock, and even in money. They have many comforts and even many luxuries in their homes. Some of them have traveled extensively, and they come back filled with awe and admiration with what the white man has done and is doing. I read the modern press, and many scientific works, and I am satisfied that man will fly in a few years more. Already the automobile is displacing the domestic animals. The telephone was a great triumph of science, next in importance to steam locomotion. But, are your people as happy with your modern methods, your crowded cities, your strenuous existence, as your forefathers were, who led the simple life? And where is this mad scramble, not for wealth alone, not for power but for mere existence, nothing more, that the human race is engaged in, going to end? Can you tell me? Take America, one of the newest civilized lands of the earth, how long will it be before her coal measures are exhausted? Her iron ores exhausted? Her forests will soon be a thing of the past. Already you hear complaints that her fertile lands are not yielding as they once did, and your population is constantly increasing. With coal gone, with iron gone, with the land poverty stricken to a point where profitable production of cereals can no longer be had, what is to become of your teeming millions?"

THE AWAKENING.

. I assured him I could not answer these questions. That I had asked myself the same things a thousand times, and no answer came to me. I handed the professor another cigar. He lit it. Just then an old Indian woman clad in a calico wrapper, but bareheaded and barefooted, came down the road towards us. She stopped some fifty feet away, and in a shy, low voice, but in good English, she called him. "Papa, did you catch me a fish for dinner?" The professor turned his head, and seeing her, said to me, "Ah, here is my guardian angel, my wife," and then to her, holding up his trout, he said, "Yes, I have it. I am coming now."

He arose, held out a dirty hand for me to shake, and in parting, said, "My dear sir, you can not imagine how much I have enjoyed our chance meeting, resulting from

your poor pronunciation of two Indian words. When you return to your civilized surroundings, ask yourself, 'Are any of this mad throng as happy as the Indian I met at the Killican'."

He joined his wife, and the aged pair passed into a brush hut beneath some stately pines. I, too, turned toward the wagon which was to carry me back to camp, meditating long and deeply on the remarks of this strolling compound of savagery and education. Environment is largely responsible for man's condition. Here was a man who had acquired considerable knowledge of the world and books, he was still a savage in his manner of life and in his habits.

His manner of talking was forceful and natural, and his command of language remarkable. The ease and abandon with which he wielded the arguments of those who rail against the existence of a Divine Being would lead one, listening to him, to imagine himself in the lecture-room of some modern university.

A GREAT DAY'S SPORT ON WAR-
NER'S RANCH.

Think of three days in the open! Three glorious days in the sunshine! "Far from the madding crowd!" Far from the rush and stir and whirl and hum of business! Far from the McNamara horror, and its sickening aftermath of jury bribing!

A short time ago, whirling over good roads and bad roads, through orange groves with their loads of fruit, rapidly assuming golden hues; through miles and miles of vineyards, now 'reft of all leaves, vineyards in which the pruners were already busily at work; past acres and acres of ground being prepared for grain; through wooded canyons and pine-screened vales; ascending from almost sea level to upwards of 3000 feet—a party of us went to Warner's Ranch after the famous canvasback ducks.

We left my home at 7:30 o'clock a. m., some of us in my machine, and two of the party in a runabout. Filled with the ambition of youth, the driver of the latter car reached Mr. William Newport's place in the Perris Valley, a run of seventy-six miles, in two hours and twenty minutes. We jogged along, reaching Newport's in three hours, and found the exultant, speed-crazed fiend waiting for us. He was loud in the praise of his speedy run. Of all of this take note a little later in the story.

We lunched with Mr. Newport, and then took him with us. What a day it was! A radiant, dry, winter day! The whole earth was flooded with sunshine. Not a cloud was in the sky. The air was full of snap and electric energy. The atmosphere absolutely clear. We wound in and out of the canyons, over dry and running streams, always ascending, climbing the eastern shoulder of Mt. Palomar, not to the top, but to a pass by which the ranch is reached.

Before 4 o'clock we were on Warner's Ranch. This property could well be described as the "Pamir" of Southern California. True, its elevation is but slight compared with the 16,000 feet of that great Asiatic country, bearing the name of "Pamir," where roams in all his freedom the true "Ovis Poli" or "Big Horn."

The ranch comprises about 57,000 acres

of land, and is the largest body of comparatively level land at even an elevation of 3500 feet in Southern California. It is an immense circular valley, rock ribbed and mountain bound. Out of it, through a narrow gorge to the southwest, flows the San Luis Rey River. The ranch is well watered. Much of it during the winter season is semi-bog or swamp land, and at all times affords wonderful grazing for stock. There are circling hills and level mesas and broad valleys here and there. Nestled between the hills are a number of mountain lakes, fed by innumerable springs around their edges. These lakes furnish food for the canvasback duck in the various grasses and other growths, of which they are extremely fond.

FIRST BAG.

Contrary to good judgment, we drove to one of these lakes, and had half an hour's shooting that evening. We got about twenty birds. We proceeded to the hotel, and after drawing our birds, hung them up where they would freeze that night and not be in the sun while we were shooting next day.

A cold north wind was blowing, which whistled mournfully through the cotton-woods, and suggested a night where plenty of blankets would be more than acceptable.

The hotel is situated at the Warner's Hot Springs, celebrated throughout all of Southern California for their wonderful curative properties. The proprietor, Mr. Stanford, and his good wife, made us comfortable, and were as accommodating as we have always found them. After a good supper we proceeded to our rooms and got ready for the next day's slaughter. Well into the night the wind whistled and blew. It finally went down. Then the temperature began to fall. The thermometer went to 29 degrees before morning. Wherever there was a thin surface of water, there was ice.

We did not get out very early. It is not necessary at Warner's. The ducks fly from lake to lake when disturbed. If too heavily bombarded they leave the valley. We breakfasted about 7 o'clock. Taking our guns and ammunition, we started out over the frosty roads for the lakes. As we reached the lower ground the frost was heavier. I found the surface of one small lake solidly frozen. At the larger lakes there was just a little ice on the edges. We distributed our men to the various lakes, and the shooting began.

[45]

Say, neighbor, did you ever hunt those big mountain canvasback? If you have, you know the story. If you have not, I am afraid I can not give you a correct impression of it. Sitting in a frozen blind, all at once you hear the whirring of wings, far off in the sky. Before you can locate the source of it, "Swish!" an old Can goes by. You look at the streak of light he leaves in the atmosphere. Then you hear another far-off alarm. You seize your gun as the gray mark passes overhead at about 125 miles an hour. You shoot at it and realize that you have shot just fifty feet behind it. Another one comes by. Bang! again goes the gun. You have done a little better this time, but you are yet not less than thirty feet in the rear. Again you try it. Just a few feathers fly. You are alarmed now, and there comes to you the admonition of an old duck hunter, who laid down the following three rules for duck shooting, viz:

"First, lead them considerably.

"Second, lead them a little more than last time.

"Third, still lead them further yet."

The next time you get your bird, a great big, magnificent Can. Kerplunk! he falls into the water, or with a dull thud, he strikes the ground with force enough to kill a horse if hit squarely by it. What a bird he was! How beautifully marked! How bright his wing! How deep his breast, compared with any other duck in the land! How magnificent the dark brown, velvet coloring of his head! How soft and satiny the white streaked back!

All over the valley the guns were booming. Out of the sky, a mile away, you would see ducks flying rapidly, suddenly crumple up and plunge to the earth or water.

DUCKS GO SKATING.

In a lull in the shooting I left my blind and went a quarter of a mile away to the little lake mentioned before as frozen over. I crept up to the top of a hill and looked down upon it. Although the sun was high in the sky, the lake was still frozen. It was surrounded by ducks. I don't want to say that they were skating on the ice. I saw one old canvasback drake, however, peck at another duck. The latter squawked and waddled out of the way, going where the water should have been. When he struck the ice, he slid for quite a little distance, balancing with his wings in a most ludicrous fashion. While cautiously watching them, I saw this performance repeated several times.

There was no hope of my approaching them within shooting distance, so I stood up to arouse the ducks, hoping to send them to my companions. They filled the air with a great clatter of wings, and circled off to various portions of the valley. I heard a great bombardment as they crossed the other lakes, and I knew that someone had taken toll from them.

It was a beautiful day, with cloudless sky. The sun's warm summerlike rays were in marked contrast to the icy breath of winter, encountered at sunrise. What a grand sunrise it was! From behind the mountains of the East, up out of the depths of the Salton Sea, Old Sol first illuminated the sky, the mountain tops and wooded ridges to the southwest and north, and then with a rich show of crimson coloring, he suddenly vaulted into the sky, touching with his golden wand each frosted leaf and frozen bush and tree, and hill and vale and mountain top.

FINE LUCK.

We shot with varying success during the morning hours.

Many of the ducks, especially the larger ones, circled high in the air like miniature aeroplanes, almost beyond human vision. How they sped on frightened wings, gradually going higher and higher, and finally darting off over the eastern rim of the valley in the direction of Salton Sea. Just before noon time my companion at one of the lakes, and myself, gathered up our ducks and hung them high in a tree at the water's edge. We then went to another lake by which the autos stood, where we had agreed to muster for lunch. The entire party were in high spirits, and pronounced the sport the best they had ever had.

After lunch two of the party in the runabout drove out of the valley to some place familiar to them. They returned later with the limit of jacksnipe—big, fat, thick-breasted, meaty looking birds.

My companion and myself returned to our blinds. The duck flight during the fore part of the afternoon was exceedingly light. I managed to land, among others, a beautiful canvasback drake. Shortly afterwards I stopped as fine a Mallard drake as I ever saw. This was the only Mallard killed on the trip.

In the gathering shadows of the coming night we drove back to the Springs. Seven guns had killed 118 ducks, fifty of them canvasback. There was a fine sprinkling of sprig, redhead, widgeon, plenty of teal, bluebills and some spoonbills, all fine, fat birds. Then there were the jacksnipe.

Tired and happy we dined. Until retiring time, we lived again the sport of the day. When we sought our beds, sleep came quickly, and I do not think any of us turned over until it was time to get up. We had packed our belongings, taken on gasoline and breakfasted, and started homeward a little after 7 o'clock.

We visited another section of the country known to one of our party, and fell in with some mountain pigeons, and in a couple of hours managed to kill sixty-eight of them. Talk about shooting! Oh, Mama! How those pigeons could fly! And pack away lead! No bird I ever saw could equal them in that particular.

Even at close range, a well-centered bird would, when hard hit, pull himself together as his feathers flew in the breeze, and sail away out into some mountain side, quite out of reach of the hunter, undoubtedly to die and furnish food for the buzzards or coyotes. We had to take awful chances as to distance in order to kill any of them.

While looking for a dead pigeon that fell off towards the bottom of a wooded bluff in some thick bunches of chapparal, I heard the quick boof! boof! of the hoofs of a bounding deer. I did not see that animal. An instant later, in rounding a heavy growth of bushes, I saw a magnificent buck grazing on the tender growth. He stood just the fraction of a second with the young twig of the bush in his mouth, looking at me with his great luminous eyes, and then he made a jump or two out of sight. Strange that these two animals had not fled at the sound of our guns.

A game warden hailed us and insisted on seeing all our hunting licenses and on counting our ducks. This privilege, under the law, we could have denied him, but we were a little proud of the birds we had, and as we were well within the number we could have killed, we made no objection to his doing so.

As a result of its speedy run the day before, the runabout had for some little time been running on a rim. We left its occupants, who disdained our help, putting on a new tire. After a beautiful run we again reached the Newport place, where we lunched. The car did not appear. We hated to go away and leave them, as we thought they might be in difficulty. We telephoned to Temecula and found they had passed that point. About two hours after our arrival they came whirling in. They had had more tire trouble. They took a hasty lunch, and we all started together.

We made the home run without incident. Spread out in one body our game made a most imposing appearance. Besides the 118 ducks there were 50 jacksnipe and 68 fine large wild pigeons.

Such days make us regret that we are growing old. They rejuvenate us—make us boys again.

BOYHOOD DAYS IN EARLY CALIFORNIA

My boyhood days, from the time I was five until I was fifteen years of age, were spent on a ranch in Yuba County, California. We were located on the east side of Feather River, about five miles above Marysville. The ranch consisted of several hundred acres of high land, which, at its western terminus, fell away about one hundred feet to the river bottom. There were a couple of hundred acres of this river bottom land which was arable. It was exceedingly rich and productive. Still west of this land was a well-wooded pasture, separated from the cultivated lands by a good board fence. The river bounded this pasture on the north and west.

In the pasture were swales of damp land, literally overgrown with wild blackberry bushes. They bore prolific crops of long, black, juicy berries, far superior to the tame berries, and they were almost entirely free from seeds. Many a time have I tem-

[53]

porarily bankrupted my stomach on hot blackberry roll, with good, rich sauce.

The country fairly teemed with game. Quail and rabbit were with us all the time. Doves came by the thousands in the early summer and departed in the fall. In winter the wild ducks and geese were more than abundant. In the spring wild pigeons visited us in great numbers. There was one old oak tree which was a favorite resting-place with them. Sheltered by some live oak bushes, I was always enabled to sneak up and kill many of them out of this tree.

I began to wander with the gun when I was but a little over eight years old. The gun was a long, double-barrel, muzzle-loading derelict. Wads were not a commercial commodity in those days. I would put in some powder, guessing at the amount, then a wad of newspaper, and thoroughly ram it home, upon top of this the shot, quantity also guessed at, and more paper. But it was barely shoved to the shot, never rammed. Sad experience taught me that ramming the shot added to the kicking qualities of the firearm. How that old gun could kick! Many times it bowled me over. St. George Littledale, a noted English sportsman, in describing a peculiarly heavy express rifle, said, "It was absolutely without recoil. Every time I discharged it, it simply pushed me over." That described my gun exactly, except that it had "the recoil." I deemed myself especially fortunate if I could get up against a fence post or an oak tree when I shot at something. By this means I retained an upright position. Armed with this gun, an antiquated powder flask, a shot pouch whose measurer was missing, and a dilapidated game bag, I spent hours in the woods and fields, shooting such game as I needed, learning to love life in the open, the trees, the flowers, the birds and the wild animals I met. I was as proud of my outfit as the modern hunter is of his $500 gun and expensive accompaniments. When I went after the cows, I carried my gun, and often got a dozen or more quail at a pot shot out of some friendly covey. If I went to plow corn, or work in the vegetable garden, the gun accompanied me, and it was sure to do deadly execution every day.

When it was too wet to plow, no matter how hard it was raining, it was just right to hunt. Clad in a gum coat, I would take my gun and brave the elements, when a seat by the fireside would have been much more comfortable. I loved to be out in a storm, to watch the rain, to hear the wind toss and tear the branches of the trees, to hear at first hand the fury of the storm, and watch the birds hovering in the underbrush, and the wild waterfowl seek the protection of the willows. In such a storm great flocks of geese would scurry across the country within a few feet of the ground. They usually went in the teeth of the gale. At such times they constantly uttered shrill cries and appeared utterly demoralized.

If there were game laws in those days, I never knew it. It was always open season with me. Often my mother would tell me to shoot something besides quail, that she was tired of them.

There was a slough on the place which was full of beaver and beaver dams. How I tried to get one of them, always without success! They were very crafty, very alert, and at the slightest indication of danger dived under water to the doors of their houses, long before one was in gunshot of them. Full many a weary hour have I spent, hidden in the brush, watching a near-by beaver dam in the hope of getting a shot,

SCORPION HARBOR, SANTA CRUZ ISLAND

but always without avail. They would appear at other dams, too far away, but never show themselves close enough to be injured.

In the winter the slough fairly swarmed with ducks of every variety. They were disturbed but little, and they used these waters as a resting place, flying far out into the grain fields and into the open plain at night for their food. The beautiful wood duck, now almost extinct in California, was very plentiful. They went in flocks as widgeon do. They would go into the tops of the oak trees and feed upon the acorns. I killed many of them as they came out of these trees. In flying they had a way of massing together like blackbirds, and one shot often brought down a goodly bag of them.

The slough I mentioned above was not a stagnant one. It was fed by water from Feather River. After winding around an island, it emptied its waters back into the river farther down stream, so that fresh water was continually entering and flowing from it. Along its banks grew a fringe of tall cottonwood trees. Many of them were completely enveloped with wild grapevines, which bore abundantly. The slough was full of two or three varieties of perch, or, as we called them, sun-fish; also a white fish called chub. These fish were all very palatable, and I caught loads of them In the fall, when the wild grapes were ripe, they would fall off into the water and were fed upon by the fish. Beneath the vine-clad cotton-woods the fishing was always good.

One afternoon I was following a path just outside of the pasture fence, through heavy wheat stubble, left after cutting time. I saw a pair of pink ears ahead of me, which I knew belonged to a rabbit. I blazed away at the ears. The gun, as usual, did execution at both ends. I went over on my back. When I regained my feet I saw a great commotion on the firing line. Rabbits' legs and feathers were alternately in the air. Investigating, I found two cottontail, one jack-rabbit and three quail in the last stages of dissolution, all the result of one shot at two rabbit's ears. I felt bigger than Napoleon ever did as I gathered up my kill and started for home.

On one of my wanderings I came across the barrel of a rifle on an Indian mound, which had been plowed up when we were preparing the land for planting. It was so coated with rust that the metal was no longer visible. Floods had covered the ground many times. Not knowing how long it had been buried there, I dug the rust and dirt out of the barrel as best I could and took it home. On my first trip to Marysville I took it to a blacksmith named Allison, who did all of our work, and asked him to cut it off about a foot from the breech end, so that I could use it as a cannon. He put it in his forge, and pulled away upon his bellows with his left hand. He held the muzzle end of the rifle barrel in his right hand, and poked at the coals with it so as to get it properly covered. He intended to heat it and then cut it off. All at once, Bang! and that horrid old thing went off. The bullet went through Allison's clothing and slightly cut the skin on his side. He was the worst scared man in all California. When he felt the sting of the bullet he threw up his hands and fell on his back, yelling lustily. I was almost as badly panic-stricken, thinking surely he was killed. I began to see visions of the gallows and the hangman's rope. He recovered his self-possession, and when he found he was not hurt, his fear turned to anger. He threw the rifle barrel out into the street, and then drove me out of the shop. When I got outside and my fear had left me, I sat down on an old wagon tongue and laughed until I was entirely out of breath. Allison came out, and my laughter must have been contagious. He leaned up against a post and laughed until he cried. His anger had left him, and we were soon fast friends again. At the proper time I ventured the opinion that the rifle could not go off again, and that it would be well enough to finish the cutting process. He consented and soon had the barrel cut off. I took the breech end home with me, and endangered my life with it many years. I generally loaded it with blasting powder, for the reason that it was usually on hand and cost me nothing, and so loaded, the cannon made more noise than had I used gunpowder.

During the campaign in which Gen. George B. McClellan ran for the Presidency against Abraham Lincoln, the Democrats of Northern California had a great celebration which lasted two or three days. Among other things was a barbecue at the race track, two or three miles out of town. Great pits were dug which were filled with oak stumps and logs, and burned for about twen-

SMUGGLERS' COVE, SAN CLEMENTE ISLAND

ty-four hours before the cooking began. These logs were reduced to a perfect bed of live coals. Over these, old-fashioned Southern negroes, of whom there were many in the neighborhood, cooked quarters of beef, whole sheep, pigs, chickens, ducks, turkeys and geese. There were at least five thousand people on the ground. My blacksmith friend, Allison, was firing a salute with an old cannon. He fired the cannon after it was loaded, with an iron rod, one end of which was kept heated in a small fire. I attended to the fire for him. After the discharge the gun was wiped out with a wet swab. The powder was done up in red flannel cartridges. Allison, with heavy, buckskin gloves on his hands, would hold his thumb over the vent or tube of the cannon. Two men, first slitting the lower end of the cartridge, would ram it into the gun. During each loading process I straddled the gun, looking towards Allison. After a number of discharges, the heat burned a hole through the glove that Allison was using, and his thumb, coming in contact with the hot metal, was withdrawn for an instant, while the assistants were sending home a charge. There was an immediate premature explosion. I

[61]

was sitting astride the gun, and felt it rise up and buck like a horse. Allison's eyes were nearly ruined, and his face filled with powder, the marks of which stayed with him the rest of his life. The two assistants were horribly mutilated, but neither of them was killed. For a time I thought I never would hear again. My ears simply shut up and refused to open for some time.

It would seem that this disaster should have been sufficient for one day, but it was not. That night there was to have been public speaking in front of the Western Hotel, by many prominent politicians. Opposite the hotel was a two-story brick building, with a veranda built around it. All of the offices on the second floor opened on this veranda. It was crowded with people. The weight became excessive. The iron posts next to the sidewalk, which sustained the veranda, slid out, and the platform swung down like a table leaf, spilling everybody onto the sidewalk. Eight or nine people were killed outright, and many more very severely injured.

When about twelve years of age I got hold of two greyhounds, sisters, named "Flora" and "Queen." During the winter time I spent much time chasing jackrabbits. In summer time the ground got so hard that the dogs would not run. The ground hurt their feet. But in the winter we had great sport. There was an immense open plain east of our property, miles long and miles wide, and level as a floor. There was a dry weed, without leaves and of a reddish color, which grew in patches all over this plain. These weed patches were the hiding places of the jackrabbits. The game was exciting and stirred one's sporting blood. I found a great difference in the speed of jackrabbits—as much in fact as in the speed of blooded horses. Occasionally I would get up one that would actually run away from the dogs, which were a fast pair. I followed the sport so persistently, and paid so little attention to fences when they interfered with my going, that I got the appellation in the neighborhood of "that d——d Graves boy."

When we got up a hare, away we went after the dogs, just as fast as our horses would carry us. The sport was hard on horseflesh, so much so that my father finally forbade me running any of our horses after the hounds.

There lived in our neighborhood a man who owned, and who had put upon the track some of the fastest horses in the State. At this time he had retired and raised horses for the fun of it. He also had some good hounds. He enjoyed the sport as much as I did. Having plenty of good horses, he furnished me with as many as I needed. We spent many days in trying to determine which of us had the best dogs. Incidentally, we wrecked some promising thoroughbreds. The question of the superiority of our dogs was never settled. We always left the door open for one more race.

Our place was the haven of all the boys of my acquaintance. When I was attending school at Marysville some boy came home with me nearly every Friday night. We would work at whatever was being done on the place Saturday forenoon, but the afternoon was ours. With the old gun we took to the pasture, hunted for game, for birds' nests and even turtles' nests. The mud turtle, common to all California waters, laid an astounding number of very hard shelled, oblong, white eggs, considerably larger than a pigeon's egg. They deposited them in the sand on the shores of the slough, covering

[64]

them up, leaving them for the sun to hatch. They always left some tell-tale marks by which we discovered the nest. Often we got several hundred eggs in an afternoon. They were very rich, and of good flavor.

There were many coons and a few wild-cats in the pasture woods. With the aid of a dog we had great sport with them. Hard pressed, they would take to the trees, from which we would shoot them. On one occasion we found four little spitfire, baby lynx, which we carried home and later traded to the proprietor of a menagerie. We got some money and two pair of fan-tail pigeons in exchange for them. When quite small they were the most vicious, untamable little varmints imaginable, and as long as we had them our hands were badly scratched by them.

On the bottom land, each year, we had a large and well assorted vegetable garden. It produced much more than we could possibly use. We boys would sell things from the garden for amusement and pin money. During one summer vacation, a boy, one Johnnie Gray, a brother of L. D. C. Gray of this city, was visiting me. We took a load of vegetables to Marysville. After sell-ing it, getting our lunch, paying for the shoeing of our horse (which in those days cost four dollars), and buying some ammunition for the gun, we had $1.50 left. We quarreled as to how we should spend this remnant. Not being able to agree, we started home without buying anything. On the outskirts of Marysville was a brewery. The price of a five-gallon keg of beer was $1.50. We concluded to take a keg home with us. It was an awfully hot summer day, and the brewer was afraid to tap the keg, thinking that the faucet would blow out under the influence of the heat before we got home. He gave us a wooden faucet, and told us how to use it. "Hold it so," he said, showing us, "hit it with a heavy hammer, watch the bung, and when you have driven it in pretty well, then send it home with a hard blow." We were sure we could do it. We drove home, put the beer in the shade by the well, spread a wet cloth over it, and then put our horse away. My parents chided us for throwing our money away on beer. In the cool of the evening we concluded to tap the keg. One of us held the faucet and the other did the driving, but we did not have the success predicted for us by the brewer.

At the critical moment we drove in the bung, but not with sufficient momentum to fasten the faucet. It flew out of our hands into the air, followed by the beer. In about a minute the keg was entirely empty. We were overwhelmingly drenched and drowned by the escaping beer, but never got a single drop of it to drink.

On another occasion some of us children were coming home from Marysville. We were driving an old white horse, named "Jake," who knew us and loved us as only a good horse can. He submitted to our abuses, shared in our pleasure and would not willingly have hurt any of us. We were in a small, one-seated spring wagon. While driving through a lane, moved on by the spirit of deviltry, one of us whipped Jake into a run, and the other one threw the reins over a fence post. The result was as could have been expected by any sane-minded individual. The horse stopped so suddenly that he sat down on the singletree, and broke both the shafts of the wagon. We were hurled out with great force, and got sundry bruises and abrasions. We wired up the shafts and got home as best we could, and, I am sorry to say, we lied right manfully as to the cause of the accident. We told a story of a drunken Mexican on horseback who chased us a considerable distance, and finally lassoed the horse, bringing him to so sudden a stop as to cause the damage. Instead of being punished, as we should have been, we were lauded as heroes of an attempted kidnapping.

One of my uncles made for us a four-wheeled wagon, the hub, spokes and axles being made out of California oak—such a wagon as you can buy in any store today, only a little larger. We made a kite of large dimensions, and covered the frame with cotton from a couple of flour sacks. At certain times of the year, the wind across the Marysville plains blew with great velocity. This kite, in a strong wind, had great pulling capacity. We would go out into the plain, put up the kite, and fasten the string to the tongue of the wagon, three or four of us pile on, and let her go. The speed that we would travel before the wind by this means was marvelous, but we tried the kite trick once too often. We got to going so fast we could not slow down nor successfully guide the wagon. It ran over an old stump, spilled us all out, and kite and wagon sailed

ARCH ROCK, SANTA CRUZ
ISLAND

CUEVA VALDEZ, SANTA CRUZ ISLAND

SANTA CRUZ ISLAND

away clear across Feather River into Sutter County and we never saw either of them again.

The boys of the present age have no such opportunities for out-of-door sports as we did in the olden days. Now it is baseball, automobile exhibitions and moving picture shows. Increased population, highpower guns, cultivation of the soil, the breaking up of large ranches into smaller holdings, have resulted in the disappearance of much of the game with which the land then abounded.

Fifty years ago in California, conditions of rural life were necessarily hard. Our habitations were but little more than shelter from the elements. We had none of the conveniences of modern life. At our house we always made our own tallow candles. We hardened the candles by mixing beeswax with the tallow. We made the beeswax from comb of the honey taken from bee trees. We corned our own beef and made sauerkraut by the barrel for winter use. We canned our own fruit, made jelly and jam from wild berries and wild grapes. We selected perfect ears of corn, shelled it at home, ran it through a fanning machine, and then had the corn ground into meal for our own consumption. We raised our own poultry and made our own butter and cheese, with plenty to sell; put up our own lard, shoulders, ham and bacon and made our own hominy. The larder was always well filled. The mother of a family was its doctor. A huge dose of blue mass, followed by castor oil and quinine, was supposed to cure everything, and it generally did. In the cities luxuries were few. To own a piano was the privilege of the very wealthy.

Speaking of pianos, in the flood of 1863, before Marysville was protected by its levee, which is now twenty-five feet high, the family cow swam into the parlor of one of the best mansions of the town, through the window. When the flood waters had subsided, she was found drowned on top of the piano.

Life under the conditions here given was necessarily hard. Our amusements were few. We, who lived in the country, had plenty of good air and sound sleep—two things often denied the city resident. Our sports were few and simple, but of such a nature that they toughened the fiber and strengthened the muscles of our bodies, thus fitting us to withstand the heavy drafts on our vitality that the hurly-burly of modern life entails upon the race.

[70]

LILY ROCK, IDYLLWILD

LAST QUAIL SHOOT OF
THE YEAR 1911

Were I musically inclined, I could very appropriately sing, "Darling, I Am Growing Old." The realization of this fact, as unwelcome as it is, is from time to time forced upon me.

On Friday, November 10, 1911, I went to the Westminster Gun Club, in an open machine, through wind and storm. Got up the next morning at 5 o'clock, had a duck shoot, drove back thirty miles to Los Angeles, arriving there at 11:30 a. m. At 1 o'clock I drove to my home, and at 2 o'clock was off for Perris Valley on a quail shoot. Had a good outing, with much hard labor. The next day I got home at half past five, completely done up.

As I went to retire, I had a good, stiff, nervous chill. So you can well see that I can no longer stand punishment, and am "growing old." As I lay there and shook, I said to myself, "Old fellow, you will soon be a 'has-been.' Your gun and fishing rod will soon decorate your shooting case as ornaments, rather than as things of utility."

Ah, well, let it be so! The memory of pleasant days when youth and strength were mine; days when the creel was full, and game limits came my way, will be with me still. I would not exchange the experience I have had with rod and gun for all the money any millionaire in the world possesses.

On my trip to the grounds of the Quail Valley Land Company, some thirty miles below Riverside, two members of the club and my wife accompanied me. We were in one of my good, old reliable Franklin cars, and from Ontario to Riverside we bucked a strong head wind that was cold and pitiless. It necessarily impeded our progress, as we had on a glass front, and the top was up, and yet we made the run of seventy-six miles in three hours and a quarter without ever touching the machine. In fact, none of the party got out of the machine, from start to finish.

The big, open fireplace at Newport's home, and the bountiful, well-cooked supper with which we were greeted, were well calculated to make us happy and contented. The long drive in the wind rendered all of us sleepy, and by 9 o'clock we had retired. I never woke up until 6 o'clock next morning.

SHOOTING GROUNDS.

After breakfast we proceeded in our machine to the shooting ground. The sky was heavily overcast with watery, wicked looking clouds. Rifts in the sky, here and there, let some frozen looking sunbeams through, but there was no warmth in their rays. We had our first shoot on the edge of a grain field, but the birds quickly flew to some high hills to the west.

Rounding the pass through these hills, I never saw the Perris Valley more weirdly beautiful. The clouds were high. On the north Mt. San Bernardino loomed up, grim, snow-capped and forbidding. To the east old Tahquitz, guardian of the passes to the desert, reared his snow-capped head, far above the surrounding country. To the south Mt. Palomar stretched his long, lazy looking form, with his rounded back and indented outline, from east to west. His distance from us made him look like a line of low, outlying hills, instead of the sturdy old mountain that he is. All of these mountains bore most exquisite purple hues. The same coloring was assumed by those groups of lesser hills that, cone-like, are scattered over the easterly edge of the Perris Valley, and

[73]

which separate the Hemet and the San Jacinto country from the rest of the valley. The coloring of the floor of the valley itself was particularly exquisite. There was just enough light, just enough of sunbeams struggling through the sodden clouds to illuminate, here and there, an alfalfa field, or here and there a grove of trees, so as to bring them out in startling contrast to the somber colors of the shaded portions of the valley. But with it were signs of the dying year, a premonition of storms to come, storms unpleasant while they last, but revivifying in their effects.

MANY QUAIL—TOO COLD.

In the fifteen years during which I have shot upon these grounds, I never got up more or larger bands of quail than we did that morning. The day was too cold for good shooting. Give me the good old summer time, with the thermometer about 80 degrees, for good quail shooting. In the cool days the birds run or get up and fly a half mile at a time. They will not scatter out and lie close, so that you can get them up one by one and fill your bags. On the cold days they also break cover at very long range. They

THE ENTRANCE AND MISSION ARCHES, GLENWOOD
MISSION INN, RIVERSIDE

led us a merry chase up the steepest hills and down the most abrupt declivities. All of the time we were slowly making good.

Lloyd Newport was there on his buckskin horse. Now you could see him way up on a hillside, then again down in some deep valley, running like mad to check the flight, or turn the running march of some band of birds that was leading those of us on foot a double-quick run. Shooting as he rode, now to the right, now to the left, then straight ahead, he got his share of the birds.

Little Fred Newport, only 14 years old, was shooting like a veteran, and long before the rest of us had scored, he proudly announced that he had the limit. The final round-up found us with 109 birds for seven guns—a good shoot, under very adverse circumstances. We had the satisfaction of knowing that we left plenty of birds on the ground for next year.

The quail shooting of 1911 is at an end. Only the memory of it remains. I shall cherish the memory deeply in my affections, and let it stir my enthusiasm for the out-of-door life when the world seems all balled up, and things are going wrong.

THE RATTLESNAKE.

While proceeding along an unfrequented road, with sage brush on each side of it, we ran across a rattlesnake, about four feet long, and of good circumference, twisted up into a most peculiar position. Investigation found that, notwithstanding the coolness of the day, he was foraging for game, and was engaged in swallowing a good-sized kangaroo rat. The tail of the rat protruded several inches from his mouth. The snake glared at us, but made no effort to escape or fight. He seemed dazed, probably half choked by his efforts to swallow the rat. We straightened him out on the ground and blew his head off with a shotgun. We then disgorged the rat, which was at least four or five inches long, and an inch and a half in diameter. The snake was then quickly skinned. He had eleven rattles and a button.

Snakes eat the eggs and the young of the quail. In view of the ravages by snakes, hawks, weasles, skunks, wildcats and coyotes I do not see how there are any quail left for the sportsmen. The fight of these marauders is constantly going on, while the sportsmen's efforts are at present limited to a very short period.

At a quarter after two we left Newport's for home. We took in a little gasoline at Riverside. This was the only stop made on the home run, which was accomplished in three hours and a quarter (seventy-six miles) with a perfect score so far as the machine was concerned.

NATURE AT HER LOVELIEST.

We did not encounter the cruel wind in returning that buffeted us on the outward trip. I never saw the San Gabriel Valley more beautiful than it was that afternoon. As we bowled along the road this side of San Dimas, the entire valley lay before us. To the west were the rugged Sierra Madre Mountains; on the east, the San Jose Hills. They connected with the Puente Hills to the south. West of these came the hills of the Rancho La Merced, running from the San Gabriel River westerly, and still west of them come the hills, which run east from the Arroyo Seco, north of the Bairdstown country. From our position these hills all seemed to connect without any breaks or passes in them. Thus the valley before us was one mountain-and-hill-bound amphitheater. The sky was overcast by grayish clouds. The sun hung low in the west, directly in front of us. How gorgeous was the coloring of the sky and valley! How the orchards and vineyards were illuminated! How the colors lingered and seemed to fondle every growing thing, and paint each rock and point of hill as no artist could! The sun hung in one position for quite a time before taking its final dip below the horizon. The clouds assumed a golden tinge, turning to burnished copper. Through breaks or irregular rifts therein, we got glimpses of the sky beyond of an opalescent blue in strong contrast with the crimson coloring of the clouds, all of which were intensely illuminated by the setting sun. Underneath this vast sea of riotous coloring there was a subdued, intense light, which I can not describe or account for. It brought every object in the valley plainly into view, lifted it into space, and illuminated it. After we had passed Azusa we chanced to look back at "Old Baldy" and the Cucamonga peaks. They were in a blaze of glorious light, purple, pink, crimson, fiery red, all mingled indiscriminately, yet all preserved in their individual intensity.

Oh, land so rare, where such visions of

HEMET VALLEY FROM FOOTHILLS ON THE SOUTH

PERRIS VALLEY GRAIN FIELD

delight are provided by the unseen powers for our delectation! As I surveyed this vast acreage, evidencing the highest cultivation, with princely homes, vast systems of irrigation, with orange orchards and lemon groves in every stage of development, from the plants in the seed beds to trees of maturity and full production, I congratulated myself on living in such an age, and amid such environments.

Let us appreciate, enjoy and defend until our dying day, this glorious land, unswept by blizzards, untouched by winter's cruel frosts, unscathed by the torrid breath of sultry summer, a land of perpetual sunshine, where roses, carnations, heliotrope, and a thousand rare, choice and delicate flowers bloom in the open air continually, where in the spring time the senses are oppressed by the odor of orange and lemon blossoms, and where the orchards yield a harvest so fabulous in returns as to be almost beyond human comprehension.

AN AUTO TRIP THROUGH THE SIERRAS.

TULE RIVER AND YOSEMITE.

I have been in California fifty-four years. During all of this time I had never visited the Yosemite. Before it was too late I determined to go there. We started in June, 1911.

Accompanied by Mrs. Graves, my son Francis and a friend, Dr. A. C. Macleish, we left Alhambra, June seventh of this year at seven o'clock a. m. We passed through Garvanza, Glendale and Tropico, and were soon on the San Fernando road. The run through the town of that name and through the tunnel, recently constructed to avoid the Newhall grade, was made in good time and without incident.

NEWHALL.

At Newhall we procured and carried with us a five-gallon can of gasoline. A short distance out of Saugus, we turned into the San Francisquito Canyon road. Shortly afterwards a brand new inner tube on the right rear wheel went completely to pieces. It had been too highly cured and could not stand the heat. We replaced it with another one, and were soon crossing and recrossing the stream which meanders down the canyon. Constantly climbing the grade, we were whirling from sunshine to shadow alternately as the road was overhung with or free from trees.

OLD MEMORIES AROUSED.

I could not help recalling my trip over the same road with my old friend, Mr. A. C. Chauvin, on the third day of October, 1876. The road was fairly good. Our machine was working nicely, the day a pleasant one, and the trip enjoyable. In a few hours we reached Elizabeth Lake. I pointed out the very spot at which Chauvin and myself camped thirty-five years before.

Ah, the fleeting years! How quickly they have sped! What experiences we have had! What pleasures we have enjoyed! What sorrows endured in thirty-five years! Well it is, that then the future was not unfolded to me, and that all the enthusiasm and hope and ambition of youth led me on to the goal, which has brought me so much joy, as well as much sorrow. Momentous events have affected not only my own life, but the life of nations in these thirty-five years.

CROSSING ANTELOPE VALLEY.

We passed the lake, turning down the grade into Antelope Valley. After several miles of very rolling country, we halted under some almond trees in a deserted orchard for lunch. The grasshoppers were thicker than people on a hot Sunday at Venice or Ocean Park in the "good old summer time." We managed to eat our lunch without eating any of the hoppers, but there wasn't much margin in our favor in the performance. Before starting we emptied our can of gasoline into the tank. Soon we intercepted the road leading from Palmdale to Fairmont and Neenach. We passed both of these places, then Quail Lake and Bailey Hotel. We were soon at Lebec. Then came the beautiful ride past Castac Lake, and down the canyon, under the noble white oak trees, which are the pride of Tejon Ranch. We passed through Ft. Tejon with its adobe buildings already fallen or rapidly falling into ruinous decay. Still descending through the lower reaches of the canyon, we took the final dip down the big grade and rolled out

ORANGE GROVES LOOKING SOUTHEAST ACROSS HEMET
VALLEY, CALIFORNIA

VIEW FROM SERRA MEMORIAL CROSS, HUNTINGTON
DRIVE, RUBIDOUX MOUNTAIN, RIVERSIDE

into the valley. A pleasant stream of water followed the road out into the plains, at which sleek, fat cattle drank, or along whose banks they lolled listlessly, having already slaked their thirst. We whirled past the dilapidated ranch buildings put down in the guide books as Rose Station. From this point, since my trip over this country a year ago, much of the road to Bakersfield has been fenced.

CLOUD EFFECTS.

While crossing Antelope Valley during the afternoon, I observed a most wonderful cloud effect. A perfectly white cloud hung over Frazier Mountain. Its base was miles long and as straight as if it had been sheared off by machinery. Its top was as irregular as its base was finished. It extended into the sky farther than the blue old mountain did above the surrounding country. Irregular in shape, it assumed the form of mountains, valleys, forests, streams, castles and turrets. I watched it for hours, apparently it never moved. It hung there as immovable as the mountain beneath it. It was at once an emblem of purity and apparent stability. After we had passed Fairmont, my attention was diverted from it for a short time, not

[83]

over ten minutes, and when again looking for my cloud, it was gone. Every vestige of it had vanished completely, and in its place was the blue sky, its color intensified by reason of its recent meager obscuration.

BAKERSFIELD.

We reached Bakersfield early in the evening, having made the run of one hundred and forty-six miles, over a heavy mountain range, on fifteen gallons of gasoline. This I call a good performance for any six-cylinder car. Coming down the Tejon Canyon, we passed the only Joe Desmond of Aqueduct fame, with some companions, taking lunch by the roadside. He had come from Mojave. He was bound for Bakersfield to buy hay.

OFF FOR PORTERVILLE.

We left Bakersfield at seven a. m. next morning, over an excellent road, for Porterville. Fifty miles after starting we picked up a nail and had a flat tire. Porterville was reached at eleven o'clock. As a side trip we were going to a camp of the San Joaquin Light & Power Company, way up on the Tule River, for the purpose of visit-

[84]

ing a grove of big trees located in that vicinity. As we had many miles of uphill work ahead of us, we concluded not to delay at Porterville for lunch. We replenished our lunch basket of the day before from a grocery store, filled our tank with gasoline and sped on. At twelve o'clock, a few miles beyond the small village of Springville, which will shortly be connected with the outside world by a railroad now in process of construction, we halted for lunch in a shady spot on one of the forks of the Tule River.

For many miles before reaching Porterville, we saw quite extensive evidence of the orange industry. There were many groves in full bearing and miles and miles of young groves but a few years planted or just set out.

TULE RIVER CANYON.

From Porterville to Springville, the canyon of the Tule River is quite wide. The course of the river itself is marked by a heavy growth of timber, some quarter of a mile in width. Orange and lemon groves have been planted in favored localities on the bench lands, here and there, but not continuously. There is much hilly land back of the canyon proper, covered with wild oats and evidently devoted entirely to pasture. Shortly after our noon halt we came to the power plant of the Mount Whitney Power Company. Here they told us our journey would end twelve miles further up the stream. From this point the canyon narrowed rapidly until it became a mere gorge. While precipitously steep, the roadbed was good. It ran along the left side of the canyon, going up. At all times we had the right hand side of the canyon in plain view. Far above us on our side, now in plain sight, now hidden by a projecting point or tall timber, was the flume of the Mount Whitney Power Company, which carried water from the river to the powerhouse we had passed. As we ascended, we continually got nearer to this flume, which was run on a grade, and at last we passed under it. We saw it shortly afterwards terminate at an intake in the canyon below our road. From here on I never enjoyed a more beautiful ride. To my mind there is nothing more attractive than a California mountain canyon and its thickly-wooded sides. Below us, foam-covered, white, radiant with light and beauty, ran the Tule River. In its rapid descent, confined to the bottom of the canyon, it

[86]

SOME BARLEY

VICTORIA AVENUE, RIVERSIDE

ROSE VALLEY

VICTORIA AVENUE, RIVERSIDE

hurtled along over water-worn boulders of great size, its swollen masses of surging waters forming here and there cascades, immense pools and miniature falls. It kept up a loud and constant roar, not too loud, but with just enough energy to be grateful to the ear.

THE CANYON A BOWER OF BEAUTY.

We had left behind us the scattering timber of the lower foothills. The sides of the canyon were clothed and garlanded in various shades of green from top to bottom. Black oak trees in their fresh, new garbs of early summer, intermingled with stately pines. All space between these trees was filled with a rich growth of all the flowering shrubs known to our California mountains. In the damper places a wild tangle of ferns and vines and bracken entirely hid the earth from view. Lilacs, white and purple, in full bloom emitted a fragrance which rendered the air intoxicating and nearly overpowered one's senses. Mingled with these bushes were the Cascara Segrada, bright-leafed maples, and the brilliantly colored stems and vividly green leaves of the Manzanitas, some in full bloom, some in berries set. The graceful red bud, found in luxuriant growth in Lake County, was also here. Likewise the elders, with their heavy clusters of yellow blossoms. The buckeye, with its long, graceful blossoms, reached far up above the undergrowth. The mountain sage, differing materially from the valley sage and bearing a yellow flower, was also here. The mountain balm, with its long purple blossoms, mingled its colors with its neighbors. Occasionally an humble thistle, with its blossom of purple base and intense pink center, thrust up its head through some leafy bower. Crowding all of these was the grease wood with its yellow bloom, the snow-bush or buckthorn, with a blossom resembling white lilac and fully as sweet, and all the other shrubs of our mountain chaparrals, all, however, blended into one beautiful and fragrant bouquet, so exquisitely formed that man's ingenuity could never equal it in arranging floral decorations. Then again a turn in the road would bring us great masses of tall dogwood with its shining leaves and beautiful white blossoms with yellow centers. They also, like the ferns, sought the cooler, darker spots. Never before have I seen the California slippery elm or leatherwood tree in such perfect form. It makes a stately branching tree. Its great yellow blossoms almost cover the limbs. The shade of the flower is a deep golden yellow. When mingled with the dogwood, the intense green of the foliage of the two trees, coupled with the white and yellow decorations, made a bouquet of rarest beauty. Thimble-berry bushes, rich in color, bright of leaf and rank of growth, sported their great white blossoms with much grace and dignity. Yellow buttercups, carnations, violets of three colors, white, yellow and purple, half hid their graceful heads under the tangled growth of various grasses by the wayside. The wild iris moved their varicolored flowers with each passing breath of air.

Hyacinths, lupins and hollyhocks were freely interspersed with the glistening foliage of the shrubbery. The tiger and yellow mountain lilies were not yet in flower, although we frequently saw their tall stems bearing undeveloped blossoms. The columbine and white and yellow clematis were much in evidence, and presented a charming picture as they wound in and out, and over and around the green leaves of the shrubs, displaying their creamy blossoms with a

[89]

dainty air and self-conscious superiority. In open places beneath the forest trees, where no large underbrush grew, a fern-like, low shrub, locally known as bear clover, completely hid the earth. It bore a white blossom with yellow center, for all the world like that of a strawberry. To my surprise, the Spanish bayonets in full bloom reared their heads above the lower growing evergreens. We saw them no further north than the Tule River canyon. What a picture the sunlight made on the mountain tops and the sloping sides of the lateral valleys of the canyon! Ah, that river, how beautiful it was! There it ran below us, in the very bottom of the canyon, ever moving, ever turbulent, ever flashing in the sunlight, ever tossing its foamy spray far up into the air, a thing of life, of joy and ecstatic force. It sang and laughed and gurgled aloud in the happiness of its life and freedom. Above was the sky, pure and radiantly blue. Its exquisite coloring was intensified by the wild riot of color beneath it. We still ascended. Each breath of air we drew was rich with the odor of pine and fir, mint and balsam. The line of survey on the opposite side of the canyon from us, marking the course of the tunnel now being constructed by the San Joaquin Light & Power Company, which terminates at a point on the mountain side at the junction of a side canyon sixteen hundred feet above the stream, was now on a level with us. We could see ahead of us where it, like the flume earlier in the day, reached the river level. At this point we knew our journey ended. We were pulling slowly up a stiff, nasty grade, when all at once a loud crash announced the demolition of some of the internal machinery of our car. We stopped from necessity.

"AUTO" BREAKS DOWN.

Our "auto" was a helpless thing. When the clutch was thrown in, it could only respond with a loud, discordant whirring. It made no forward movement. We all thought our differential had gone to smash. One of our party went on ahead, and at a nearby camp we telephoned Mr. Hill, superintendent of the power company, of our predicament. He directed a man who was working a pair of heavy horses on a road near by, to hitch onto us and haul us up to his place, a mile or so distant. All of us, except Mrs. Graves, and our chauffeur, who had to steer the car and work the brakes, walked. It was slow going, but the journey finally ended. We found a good, clean camp, clean beds and a good supper awaiting us. That night we reaped the sweet repose which comes from exertion in the open air.

Early next morning we blocked up our car and took off the rear axle, uncoupled the differential case and found everything there intact. We then removed the caps from the wheel hubs and took out the floating axles, or drive shafts. One of them was broken into two pieces. It either had a flaw in it when made or had crystallized, no one could determine which. We got Los Angeles by phone, ordered the necessary parts by express to Porterville, and, think of it, we had these parts delivered to us at two o'clock the next afternoon!

THE SODA SPRING.

We spent the rest of Friday, June ninth, in visiting a magnificent soda and iron spring, a mile above camp, which is for all the world like the spring of the same quality in Runkle's Meadows, above the lake on Kern River, some ninety miles above Kernville. The waters of the spring were deliciously cool and refreshing.

[92]

A ROCKY STREAM

A TRAMP UP A MOUNTAIN.

Next morning the male members of our party started up a steep mountain trail to see some sequoias I had heard about. Unused as we were to excessive exercise and the altitude, the climb was a hard one. We ascended from four thousand feet elevation to over seven thousand feet. Most of the way the trail was through heavy fir and sugar-pine. Going up we ran into two beautiful full-grown deer, a buck and a doe. They fled to security with easy, graceful jumps, into the thick underbrush. We heard grouse drumming loudly in two or three different localities and saw one bird make a long dive from one pine tree to another. We found wild flowers in profusion, of the same variety, fragrance and coloring as encountered in the canyon the day before. Just as we reached the summit, we found, standing on the backbone of the ridge—so located that rain falling on it would flow from one side of it into one water-shed, and from the other side into another water-shed—a great, stately sequoia gigantea fully three hundred feet high and of immense circumference. There wasn't a branch on it within one hundred feet of the ground. It was in good leaf, except at the top, which was gnarled and weather-beaten. Its base had been cruelly burned. This tree bears a striking resemblance to the grizzly giant which we saw later in the Mariposa big tree grove near Wawona. Not far from this fine old guardian of the pass, were groups of noble trees, fully as tall, but not as large as the one described, but perfect trees, erect, stately, and imposing. The bark of all of these trees was very smooth and very red, much more highly colored than the trees in the Wawona grove.

I was too much fatigued to make another mile down the west side of the mountain (we had come up from the east) to inspect a much larger grove of still larger trees. Two of the younger members of our party, my son Francis and Harry Graves, our chauffeur, made the trip while Dr. Macleish and I awaited their return on the summit. They came back enthusiastic over the lower groves, the trees there being much more numerous in number and much larger in size than the ones we first ran into. We sat around resting a while, straining our necks looking for the tops of those trees, all of which were way up there in the blue sky. We wondered how many years they had been there, and what revolutions in climate and topographical appearance of the country they had witnessed. Finally, having satiated ourselves with their beauty, we started on the return journey, which was made without incident, except that we disturbed a hen grouse with a fine brood of little ones about the size of a valley quail.

A MOTHER GROUSE.

The mother bird flew into a scrub oak. She there asserted the privilege of her sex and scolded us in no uncertain tones. When all her young had flitted away to cover, still scolding, she took one of those long dives down to a deep dark canyon, flying with incredible rapidity, and apparently not moving a feather. No other bird I ever saw can do the trick as a grouse does it. We saw but few other birds on this excursion. An occasional blue-jay, a vagrant bee-bird, now and then a robin, and once in a while a most brilliantly colored oriole made up the list. Fluffy-tailed gray squirrels chattered at us noisily from the wayside trees. They seemed bubbling over with life and motion. We stopped at the Soda Springs for a life-giving draught of its refreshing waters, and were back to camp in time for lunch.

FLIGHT OF LADY-BUGS.

When we reached the Soda Springs, we met the most remarkable migration of red lady-bugs that I ever saw. They were coming in myriads from down the main canyon and each side canyon. They extended in a swarm from the ground to a distance above it of from ten to twelve feet. Huge rocks would be covered six or eight inches deep with them. Occasionally they would light upon a tree, and in a few moments the tree or bush would be absolutely covered, every speck of foliage hidden. It was difficult to breathe without inhaling them, and we were kept busy brushing them from our faces and clothes. They were all traveling in one direction—down stream. I believe that they had been into the canyons laying their eggs, and were returning to the valleys. All afternoon the flight continued, but by nightfall there wasn't a lady-bug in sight.

We tried fishing, but the water was too high and too turbulent for success in the sport.

AUTO REPAIRS ARRIVE.

About two o'clock that afternoon our new floating axle and fittings had arrived, and

[96]

in another hour the car was set up and ready for business.

The following morning (Sunday) we bade Mr. Hill and his men good-bye and started for Crane Valley. The drive out of the canyon was a beautiful one. We did not go all the way to Porterville, but went several miles beyond Springville, turned into Frazier Valley, and went to Visalia by way of Lindsay and half a dozen small villages, and from there on to Fresno, which place we reached at about two o'clock. The ride was a hot one. We drove through miles and miles of orange orchards, some in full bearing, but mostly recently planted.

FRESNO.

We left Fresno at about four-thirty o'clock over the same road we traveled a year before. However, before crossing the river, we turned to the right and went up through a town, Pulaski, where we crossed on a splendid cement bridge. The road was pretty badly cut up from heavy teaming, but we got to Crane Valley about ten o'clock p. m. We had considerable trouble with our carburetor during the afternoon, and lost much time trying to locate the trouble, but without avail.

The younger members of the party, although the hour was late, went to prowling around the camp for something to eat. They raided the cook's pie counter in the dark. We had had a splendid lunch at Fresno at two o'clock, and Mrs. Graves and I were too tired to want anything to eat, and retired on our arrival.

CRANE VALLEY.

Since our visit to Crane Valley a year ago, we found that the then uncompleted dam was finished. Instead of a small reservoir of water, we found a vast inland sea, with water one hundred and ten feet deep at its deepest part. It is six miles long, by from half to one mile in width. It is twenty-five miles in circumference. The dam proper is nearly two thousand feet long, and at one part is one hundred and fifty-four feet high on its lower side. It is built with a cement core, with rock and earth fill, above and below; that is, on each side of the cement work. The inner and outer surface of the dam are rock-covered. To give you an idea of its capacity, if emptied on a level plain, its waters would cover forty-two thousand acres of land one foot deep. When we were there a discharge gate had been open two weeks, discharging a stream of water two and one-half feet deep, over a weir thirty-eight feet wide, and the surface of the reservoir had been lowered but two inches. I say, "All hail to the San Joaquin Light & Power Company and its enterprising officials, for the great work completed by them." It is a public benefactor in storing up, for gradual discharge, at a time of the year when it could do no good, this vast body of water which would otherwise run to the sea.

What a place for rest are these mountain valleys! After inspecting the dam, catching some bass and killing a rattlesnake, we were all contented to sit around for the remainder of the day. A certain languor takes possession of the human frame when one has come from a lower to a higher altitude. One ceases to think, his mentality goes to sleep, he can doze and dream and be happy in doing so.

AGAIN ON THE ROAD.

Tuesday morning, leaving Mr. Dougherty, the Superintendent, and his good wife, we started for Wawona. We traveled up the left side of the lake, over a good road, above the water level, to its extreme western end. Here we climbed a mountain to an elevation of five thousand five hundred feet, over a cattle trail which was badly washed out, to a road leading to Fresno Flats. This place we soon reached over a good but steep road-bed.

Then, winding in and out of the canyon through a foothill country, we made steady progress until we reached the main road from Raymond to Wawona. The grade was uphill all the time. We left the lumbering camp known as Sugar Pine to our right. The lumber interests have made a sad spectacle of miles and miles of country, recently heavily forested. There seems to be no idea in the lumberman's mind of saving the young growth when cutting the larger timber. All the young growth is broken down and destroyed, and finally burned up with the brush and wreckage of the larger trees, leaving the mountain side scarred and blackened, and so lye-soaked that immediate growth of even brush or chaparral is impossible. We passed through Fish Camp, and in a short time came to the toll-gate at which point the road to the Mariposa Grove of big trees branches off.

FERN BRAKES FOUR FEET IN HEIGHT AT PINE HILLS

CALIFORNIA WHITE OAK

WAWONA.

The rest of the run to Wawona was all downhill, through heavy timber, over a good but dusty road. We reached the hotel in time for lunch. That afternoon, with Mr. Washburn, we took a drive of some miles around the Big Meadows, near the hotel, went up the river and took in all points of interest in the neighborhood. Wawona Hotel is pleasantly located. It is an ideal place to rest. There inertia creeps into the system. You avoid all unnecessary exercise. You are ever ready to drop into a chair, to listen to the wind sighing through the trees, to hear the river singing its never ending song, to watch the robins and the black birds and the orioles come and go, and observe the never-ending coming and going of guests. Some are just arriving from the San Joaquin valley, some are departing to it, or coming home or going to the Yosemite, or starting off or coming from the Big Trees or Signal Peak. You eat and sleep and forget the cares of life, forget its troubles, and smelling the incense of the pines, sleep comes to you the moment your head touches your pillow and lasts unbrokenly until breakfast-time the next day.

LOS ANGELES PEOPLE KNOWN EVERYWHERE.

We took passage on a stage-coach next morning for the Wawona big trees. The trip is one ever to be remembered. The road winds around over the mountains, always ascending, for about eight miles. The great trees are scattered over quite an expanse of territory. A technical description of them would be out of place here. To realize their size and majesty you must see them. Many are named after prominent men of the nations, and after various cities and states of the Union. I was glad to see the names of Los Angeles and Pasadena on two magnificent specimens. We drove through the trunk of a standing tree, and present herewith a picture of the feat. The gentleman on the left on the rear seat is a Mr. Isham, and the lady and gentleman on the same seat are a Mr. and Mrs. Risley, just returned from a trip around the world. They are from the same city in the east as Dr. and Mrs. W. Jarvis Barlow, and Mrs. Alfred Solano of this city, to whom they desired to be warmly remembered. Go where you will, you meet someone who knows someone in Los Angeles.

We lunched in the open air at the big

trees, and made the return trip in a reverent mood, almost in silence, each of the party given over to his or her reflections. I realize that there is in my mind an ineffaceable mental picture of those gigantic trees, which are so tall, so large, so impressive and massive that they overpower the understanding.

During our stay at Wawona we tried fishing in the main river, which was swollen to a raging torrent by the melting snows. We found it so discolored and so turbulent that fishing was not a success. We also visited the cascades. An immense body of water comes down a rocky gorge very precipitously. From one rock to another the water dashes with an awful roar. Mist and spray ascend and fall over a considerable area, keeping the trees and brush and grass and ferns dripping wet, and it would soon render one's clothing exceedingly uncomfortable.

WE GO TO YOSEMITE BY STAGE.

It is twenty-six miles from Wawona to Yosemite Valley. The stages leave Wawona at eleven thirty a. m. to make the trip. On June sixteenth we took our places with some other victims of this piece of transportation idiocy, on an open four-horse stage for

Yosemite. The going was very slow. It was hot and dusty, and we soon got irritable and uncomfortable. Why the traveling public should be subjected to this outrage is beyond me. We ground our weary way over the dusty road, oblivious to the scenery, until six o'clock, when we suddenly came to Inspiration Point, our first view of the great Valley.

YOSEMITE VALLEY.

The beauty of the scene to some extent compensated us for a beastly ride. Beyond us lay the great gorge known as the Yosemite. Below us the Merced River. On the left were Ribbon Falls, and just beyond them El Capitan. On our right, but well in front of us, were the Bridal Veil Falls. We were just in time to see that wonderful rainbow effect for which they are celebrated. Surely no more beautiful sheet of water could be found anywhere. A wonderful volume of water dashes over the cliff, unbroken by intercepting rocks, and drops a straight distance of six hundred feet. Then it drops three hundred feet more in dancing cascades to the floor of the valley and divides up into three good-sized streams which empty into the Merced River. When once started on its downward course, the water seems all spray. At the bottom of the first six-hundred-foot descent it made a mighty shower of mist like escaping steam from a giant rift in some titanic boiler, and soon reached the floor of the valley. The road from El Portal comes up on the north side of the river. We passed El Capitan, which rears its massive head three thousand three hundred feet in the distance, perpendicularly above the river. We were shown the pine tree, one hundred and fifty feet high, growing out of a rift in the rocks on its perpendicular face, more than two-thirds of the distance from its base. The tree looked to us like a rose bush, not two feet high, in a garden.

As we proceeded up the Valley there were pointed out to us the Three Brothers, a triple group of rocks, three thousand eight hundred feet high. Cathedral Spire, Sentinel Rock, Yosemite and Lost Arrow Falls, and all the other points of interest that can be seen on entering the Valley.

The river was abnormally high—higher we were told, than it had been in many years. It flowed with great rapidity, as if hurrying out of the valley to join the flood waters

which had already submerged many acres of
land in the San Joaquin valley, miles below.
It looked dark and wicked, as if it carried
certain death in its cold embrace. Half of
the Yosemite valley was flooded. Meadows,
rich in natural grasses, were knee deep with
back water.

We reached the Sentinel Hotel, and
sloughing off the most of the fine emery-like
mountain dust with which we were enveloped, we got our first good look at the Yosemite Falls. They were at their best.
Imagine a large river, coming over a cliff,
a seething, foaming mass of spray, and drop-
ping, in two descents, two thousand six hundred and thirty-four feet, sending heaven-
ward great clouds of mist! I took one look,
then looked up the Valley to the great Half
Dome, to Glacier Point, from there to Sentinel Peak and the Cathedral Spires, and I
concluded that the Yosemite is too beautiful
for description, too sublime for comprehension and too magnificent for immediate human understanding. In the presence of
those awful cliffs, towering, with an average
height of over three thousand feet, above the
floor of the valley; those immense waterfalls, as they thundered over the canyon

ANOTHER VIEW OF SPRING CREEK

walls; that mad river, gathering their united flow into one embrace, scurrying away with an irresistible energy that almost sweeps you off your feet as you look at it, all things human seem to shrink into the infinitesimal. You do not ask yourself, "How did all this get here?" You accept the situation as you find it. You leave it to the scientists to dispute whether the valley was formed wholly by glacial action or by some gigantic convulsion of nature, which tore its frowning cliffs apart, leaving the Valley rough, unfinished and uncouth to the gentle, molding hand of Time to smooth it up and beautify its floor with its present growth of oaks and pines and shrub and bush and ferns and vines, and laughing, running waters.

You are four thousand feet above sea-level. All around you cliffs and walls tower three thousand feet and upwards above you. Back of these are still higher peaks, whole mountain ranges, clothed in their snowy mantles, this season far beyond their usual time. The air is delightful, pure as the waters of the Yosemite Falls, soft as a carpet of pine needles to the foot-fall, balmy as the breath of spring, and cool and invigorating.

THE VALLEY OVERFLOWING WITH VISITORS.

The valley is full of people; the hotels crowded, the camps overflowing. From early dawn until the setting summer sun has cast long shadows over meadow and stream alike, there is a moving mass of restless people, either mounted on horseback, in vehicles or on foot, going out or coming in from the trails and side excursions. The walker seemed to get the most fun out of life. Man and woman are alike khaki clad and sunburned to a berry-brown. They walk with the easy grace of perfect strength and long practice, and think nothing of "hiking" to the top of Yosemite Falls or Sentinel Peak and back. One of the favorite trips is to Glacier Point by the Illilouette, Vernal and Nevada Falls, a distance of eleven miles, remaining there all night at a comfortable inn and returning by a shorter route by Sentinel Peak.

Looking up between the rocky walls of the valley, how far away the stars all looked at night! In that pure atmosphere, how beautiful the sky! How perfect each constellation! Each star with peculiar brightness shone. One's view of the sky is circumscribed by the height of the cliffs. Instead of the great arched vault of heaven one usually looks up to, one sees only that part of the sky immediately above the valley. It was like looking at the heavens from the bottom of a deep, narrow shaft. I looked in vain for well known beacon lights. They were not in sight. The towering cliffs shut them out. The sky looked strange to me, yet how beautiful it was! Through the gathering darkness we took one more look at the Yosemite Falls and betook ourselves to bed, to sleep the sleep once enjoyed in the long ago, when as children we returned, tired but happy, from some long outing in the woods.

WE VISIT THE FLOOR OF THE VALLEY.

On the following morning we took in the sights of the floor of the valley. We rode to Mirror Lake, which, however, did not come up to its reputation. This summer the entrance to the lake has changed its channel from its west to its east side, and a long sand bar has been deposited in the lake proper, all of which our guide told us marred the reflections usually visible therein.

We passed hundreds of people of all ages walking through the valley. In visiting the Yosemite you do not realize that the valley

is several miles long, and has an average
width of about one-half a mile. The great
height of the surrounding walls dwarfs your
idea of distance. Even the trees, many of
which are of great size, look small and puny.

THE HAPPY ISLES.

We drove to the Happy Isles, small islands
covered with trees, around which the river
surges in foaming masses. Standing at the
upper end of the one of the Happy Isles,
one gets a splendid impression of the cas-
cade effect of the waters, rushing madly
down a steep rocky channel, with an irresistible, terrifying force. The descent of the
bed of the stream is very marked. The waters come over submerged, rocky masses.
Just as you think that maddened torrent
must sweep over the island, engulfing you
in its course, the stream divides, half of it
passing to the right, and half to the left.
These divided waters unite again farther
down the valley.

On our return from this short excursion,
Francis, Dr. Macleish and Harry, taking
their lunch with them, walked up to the top
of the Yosemite Falls. They stood beneath
the flag at Yosemite Point and got a compre-

HARVESTING IN SAN JOAQUIN VALLEY

hensive view of the entire valley. They reported the trip a heart-breaking one.

MILITARY GOVERNMENT.

The valley has a military government. What Major Forsyth says goes. There are no saloons in the Yosemite, nor are there any cats. The Major saw a cat catch a young gray squirrel. He issued an edict that the cats must go or be killed. They went.

EXCURSION TO GLACIER POINT.

The next day all of our party, except Mrs. Graves, who had made the journey some years before, went to the top of Glacier Point. We took a stage to the Happy Isles and there mounted mules for the trail. The climb is a steady one. Soon we got our first view of the Vernal Falls. To my mind they are the most perfect waterfalls in the Valley. The water flows over the cliffs an unbroken mass, one hundred feet wide. The initial drop is three hundred and fifty feet. The effect can not be imagined by one who has not seen the actual descent of this great mass of water. The emerald pond above the falls, in which the waters assume an emerald hue, and appear to seek a momentary rest before taking the final plunge over the cliffs, is one of the Valley's beauty spots. The roar of the falling waters, striking the rocks below, is loud and reverberating. Great clouds of spray and mist float off in falling masses, appearing more like smoke than water.

After passing Vernal Falls you come to the Diamond Cascades. They are below the Nevada Falls. The long flowing waters from the Nevada Falls have cut a channel deep into the bed rock. You cross this channel on a bridge. Under and below the bridge the water flows with such velocity that great volumes of it are hurled into the air in long strings, one succeeding the other. The sunlight on these strings of water makes them flash like diamonds. The effect is as if some one were sowing diamonds by the bushel above the water. A similar effect is noticed, though not so pronounced, just above the Nevada Falls. The latter are something like a mile above Vernal Falls. They are six hundred feet high. They seem to come over the cliff like the Yosemite Falls, through a broken or distorted lip, and the water is lashed to foam and looks for all the world like the smoke of some mighty conflagration,

[112]

upon which a score of modern fire engines are playing. Near the top of the Nevada Falls is a fir tree more than ten feet in diameter, said to be the largest tree in the Yosemite Valley. Just above the falls we again crossed the river on a bridge. Near the bridge, on the rocks is plain evidence of glacial scourings. A glacial deposit is left in patches on the rocks which is today as smooth as plate glass.

ABANDONED EAGLE'S NEST.

Above Vernal Falls we skirted the base and climbed partly around the side of Liberty Cap, one of the great granite domes of the valley, until we reached the top of the cliff over which the Nevada Falls plunge. Well up on the side of this cliff, in an inaccessible retreat, our guide, who had traversed this route for twenty-two years, showed me an ancient but now abandoned eagle's nest. The noble birds, in late years, not liking the coming of the thousands of excursionists who passed that way daily, forsook their home for some other locality.

The trail now winds around the mountainsides, finally crossing the canyon above the Illilouette Falls. In a short time we are at

Glacier Point. As you go out to the iron railing erected on the outer edge of a flat rock on the extreme edge of the cliff, and look down into the valley below you, you can not help a shrinking feeling, and you are only too glad soon to move back and get a view from safer quarters.

OVERHANGING ROCK.

The celebrated overhanging rock is at this point. It is a piece of granite, say four or five feet wide, flat on top, but with rounding edges. It sticks out from the cliff several feet. Foolhardy people walk out to the edge of it and make their bow to imaginary audiences over three thousand feet below. One of the guides with our party, wearing heavy "chaps" (bear-skin overalls) walked out upon this rock, took off his hat, waved it over his head, posed for his photograph, even took a jig step or two, stood on one foot and peered into the abyss below with apparent unconcern. Earlier in life I might have taken a similar chance, but it would be a physical impossibility for me to do it now. We feasted our eyes on the magnificent view.

We were now nearly level with the Half Dome (our elevation was seven thousand one

NEVADA FALLS ROM GLACIER
POINT UPPER YOSEMITE

NEVADA FALLS, CLOS
RANGE YOSEMITE FAI

hundred feet), below us the beautiful valley
with its winding river, bright meadows and
stately forests. Horses staked out on the
meadow looked like dogs; people, like ants.
The Yosemite, Vernal, Nevada and Illilouette Falls, Mirror Lake, the roaring cascades
above, the Happy Isles, all the peaks of the
upper end of the Valley, and mountains for
miles and miles beyond, snow-capped and
storm-swept, were in plain sight.

After an appetizing lunch at the hotel, we
took the short trail for the valley. It is
three and a half miles long, almost straight
up and down, and is hard riding or walking.
But the journey was soon ended, and that
night we again slept the sleep of the joy-
ously tired.

Morning came too soon, ushering in another perfect mountain day. We simply
loafed around, never tiring of looking at the
river or falls in sight, or the everlasting
cliffs above us. We put in an hour or two
watching a moving-picture outfit photo-
graphing imitation Indians.

VIEWS THROUGH A "CLAUDE LORRAINE GLASS."

That evening as the daylight waned, while
sky and stream, trees, mountains and jagged
peaks were still gloriously tinted with the

sun's last rays, Mr. Chris. Jorgenson, the artist, brought out a "Claude Lorraine glass." We stood upon the bridge of the Merced river and caught upon the glass the Half Dome, bathed in mellow light; the Yosemite Falls with its great mass of falling waters exquisitely illuminated; Sentinel Peak, the swiftly moving river fringed with green trees, the grassy meadows and the fleecy clouds. The picture of reflected beauty so produced, such tints and colors, such glints of stream and forest, such a glorified reproduction of the beauties of the Valley can only be imagined, they can not be described.

There were enough Los Angeles people in the Yosemite at the time to have voted a bond issue. They were all out for a good time, and were having it.

OUR RETURN TO WAWONA.

Not wishing to undergo the torture of the noon-day ride back to Wawona, a party of us chartered a stage to leave the Valley at six o'clock a. m. We got off next morning at six-forty and had a delightful drive, making Wawona before noon. Thus a few hours' difference in the time of starting made a pleasure of what otherwise would have been a torment. While we were in the Valley some Los Angeles friends had arrived at Wawona and were in camp near the hotel.

SIGNAL PEAK.

We rested at Wawona several days. During one of these I went with the boys on horseback to Signal Peak, whose elevation is seven thousand and ninety-three feet. The San Joaquin valley was enveloped in haze, but the mountain ranges east of us were in plain sight. We could see all the peaks from Tallac at Lake Tahoe to Mt. Whitney. Mt. Ritter, Mt. Dana, Mt. Hamilton, Galen Clarke, Star King, Lyell, the Gale Group, and others whose names I do not now recall, stood out in bold relief, encased in snowy mantles. The view from Signal Peak is well worth the trip. We enjoyed it so much that we persuaded Mrs. Graves and some ladies to take it next day by carriage, which is easily done.

On June twenty-third the boys went to Empire Meadows, some eleven miles distant, with a fishing party. They had fair luck, the entire party taking nearly two hundred eastern brook trout.

HOMEWARD BOUND.

On the morning of June twenty-fourth, at six o'clock, we started on our homeward journey. We had carburetor trouble coming up—we still had it going out, until at last our driver discovered that one of the insulating wires had worn through its covering and, coming in contact with metal, had resulted in a short circuit. When this was remedied our troubles were over, and our machine performed handsomely. The first forty-four miles to Raymond were all downhill, over a very rough road, with sharp turns and depressions every one hundred feet or so, to allow the rain-water to run off of the road, which rendered the going very slow. We were three hours and a half reaching Raymond. Passing this point we sped into Madera, then to Firebaugh. During the morning we saw a stately pair of wild pigeons winging their swift flight in and out of some tall pine trees.

WATER HIGH IN SAN JOAQUIN VALLEY.

The San Joaquin river was very high and had overflowed thousands of acres of land. Our road, slightly elevated, passed for miles through an inland sea. To reach Los Banos, we made a wide detour to the left. We

CEDAR CREEK AT PINE HILLS

SCENE NEAR PINE HILLS LODGE

crossed the Pacheco Pass into the Santa Clara valley. We had intended to go to Hollister by way of San Felipe. Some three miles from the latter place we saw a sign reading "Hollister nine miles." We took the road indicated and must have saved six or seven miles.

HOLLISTER.

This portion of the country is largely given over to fruit growing and raising flower and garden seed, acres and acres of which were in full bloom, and the mingled colors were exceedingly charming. We reached Hollister in good time, one hundred and seventy miles from Wawona. We found good accommodations at the Hotel Hartman. Bright and early next morning we were off. We went due west. We found the bridge over the Pajaro river utterly destroyed by last winter's rains. We crossed through the bed of the stream without difficulty and were soon upon the main road to Salinas, just below San Juan. As we ascended the San Juan hills, we paused at a turn in the road and got a view of the beautiful valley in which Hollister lies. No more peaceful landscape ever greeted mortal eye. Every acre as far as one could see, not devoted to pasturage, was cultivated. There were grain and hay fields, orchards by the mile, and the seed farms in full bloom, while cattle and horses grazed peacefully in many pastures. We turned away with regret at leaving a land so beautiful, so happy and contented looking.

"THE FERRYMAN."

At Salinas river we found a man with a good-sized team of horses, who, for one dollar and fifty cents, hauled us through a little water which we could have crossed without difficulty, and a quarter of a mile of loose, shifting sand which we could never have crossed without his aid. He has a tent in which he has lived since last winter, and he gets them "coming and going," as no machine can negotiate that stretch of road unassisted. He earns his money, and I wish him well.

FINE RUN TO LOS OLIVOS.

Taking out the time spent at lunch and in taking on gasoline, we reached Los Olivos, two hundred and thirty-one miles from Hollister, in eleven hours' running time. We again had good accommodations at Los Olivos and were off next morning on the final "leg" of our journey. The road from the north side of Gaviote Pass to within a few miles of Santa Barbara is a disgrace to Santa Barbara county. I prefer the valley route with its heat to the coast route, and I warn all automobilists to avoid the latter route.

We had a good lunch at Shepherd's Inn, and then ran home in time for dinner. We came by Calabasas, and just before we reached the Cahuenga Pass we turned off and went through Lankershim on our way to Alhambra. We all remarked that in no section of the state we had visited did the trees look as healthy, the alfalfa as luxuriant, the garden truck as vigorous, as they did at Lankershim. Every inch of the ground there is cultivated; there are no waste spots.

"HOME AGAIN."

Home looked better and dearer to us when we reached it than it ever did before. We had traveled one thousand and forty-five miles and used on the trip one hundred and four gallons of gasoline, thus averaging over all sorts of roads, including several mountain ranges, a little better than ten miles to the gallon. I defy any six cylinder car in America to beat this record. I used the same old Franklin car, in which I have made four tours of California. I have no apology to offer for breaking the drive-shaft. The parts of any car will stand just so much. Pass this point and trouble ensues. This grand old car has run over eighty thousand miles and seen much hardship. I salute it!

THE END.

Lightning Source UK Ltd.
Milton Keynes UK
UKHW021459030219
336610UK00006B/160/P